1/1 ✓ **P9-DML-269**
OLS

$23.00

MARSHLANDS

MARSHLANDS

MATTHEW OLSHAN

FARRAR, STRAUS AND GIROUX

NEW YORK

Farrar, Straus and Giroux
18 West 18th Street, New York 10011

Copyright © 2014 by Matthew Olshan
All rights reserved
Printed in the United States of America
First edition, 2014

Library of Congress Cataloging-in-Publication Data
Olshan, Matthew.
   Marshlands / Matthew Olshan. — First edition.
      pages   cm
   ISBN 978-0-374-19939-5 (hardcover)
   1. Physicians—Fiction.   2. Treason—Fiction.   I. Title.

PS3615.L732 M38 2014
813'.6—dc23
                                                    2013034005

Designed by Jonathan D. Lippincott

Farrar, Straus and Giroux books may be purchased for educational, business,
or promotional use. For information on bulk purchases, please contact the
Macmillan Corporate and Premium Sales Department at 1-800-221-7945,
extension 5442, or write to specialmarkets@macmillan.com.

www.fsgbooks.com
www.twitter.com/fsgbooks • www.facebook.com/fsgbooks

1   2   3   4   5   6   7   8   9   10

For SWO

I

1

Early on, he kept a journal, but there was nowhere to hide the paper scraps. They disinfected his cell once a week. He returned from the yard to find every crevice blasted clean, the floor puddled with bleach.

The cleaning left a residue on the walls, so he took to writing in that alkaline dust, tracing letters with a burning fingertip, knowing his work would be scoured away at the end of the week. Still, it was work. Erasure was the fate of all written words. Books eventually moldered and disintegrated. Even the ancient shards he used to collect on hunting trips in the marshes eventually succumbed to sun and sand, the maker's marks becoming fainter and fainter until they vanished.

Nevertheless, he observed; he wrote. The point was to get it down. His writing was a source of amusement to the guards, who called it "finger painting." They came in and altered words as he was writing them, changing "hunt" to "cunt," or "cape gun" to "rape gun," adding cartoons, sometimes even caricatures of him.

There was one guard whose caricatures were uncanny. It was a marvel that crude lines could be so pregnant with truth. He spent many long nights contemplating the artistic superiority of that guard, a prankster who once pissed in his open mouth while he slept.

He came to prefer the caricatures to his own ramblings. He

encouraged the guard to draw more, but it only led to beatings. He lost several teeth to the man's talented baton.

Then one day he returned from a work detail to find the walls of his cell gleaming with paint. The chemical odor frightened him. The cell, which had been painfully bright before, was blinding now. The new paint dried into a kind of armor. Cleanings no longer left a dusty residue. Now it was impossible to write; therefore, there was nothing to be said.

He missed his old walls. *What is this?* he asked, tapping the paint with a long fingernail, but instead of answering his question, they told him that his parents were dead. Or perhaps they said his parents were dead to him.

In any case, it was time to go home.

He had no idea what they were talking about. His cell was his home. He'd made up his mind to die there. There was a kind of symmetry to it. This sunbaked country had stolen his life, and he was looking forward to stealing it back. He was saving bits of thread toward that day, secretly braiding a slender rope.

They made him shower and comb his hair. Afterward, they sat him in a room with a stack of magazines and told him to read up on current events. Some of the magazines were crumbling with age, and even those were filled with futuristic wonders. He found himself lingering over photographs of food. Food and bathrooms. Dinner tables had gotten to look like beds heaped with full-bodied women; bathroom fixtures shone like weapons of war.

They handed him a paper bag with his effects. Beetles had gotten to the wallet, which crumbled in his fingers. There was a watch, but no watchband. He didn't recognize the watch; its face was cracked, the time frozen. He tried to give it to one of his minders, but the man shook his head and handed it back.

His uniform had somehow survived, but the voluminous trousers swallowed him up. Years of unrelenting heat had rendered every ounce of fat from his body. He was ashamed of his skeletal hips, of the fabric at his waist that could be gathered in two fists. The generous cut of the jacket—his old size!—felt like a rebuke, another measurement of his fall.

Someone wanted the uniform as a souvenir, so he traded it for clothes more in keeping with his station, a scorched cook shirt and torn houndstooth slacks, discards from the prison laundry. It was a good trade. He wasn't a doctor anymore, much less an officer. He was a disgrace; even so, he wished he could wear the uniform, if only as a hair shirt, a badge of shame.

On the way to the airstrip, they told him the black hood was for his own protection. There had been death threats. In the same breath, they told him not to count on government protection.

The amount of anger in their voices astonished him. These were young men. They would have been children at the time of his trial, perhaps not even born.

He was led up a ramp and into the hold of a cargo plane, where they chained him to a metal chair by the waist and ankles. The tight blindfold underneath his hood provided for total darkness; the deafening roar of the engines made his isolation complete.

During the flight, the changes in pressure reminded him of one of his first guards, an amateur boxer whose favorite punishment was a cupped blow to the ears. Still, he was glad of the earache, despite the pain. The way it came and went was proof that time wasn't standing still.

A day passed. Perhaps two. There were stops for refueling. At each stop, a few soldiers would bribe their way onto the plane. As the thunder in his ears gradually died down, he'd hear camera sounds, followed by laughter and loud talk as bills surreptitiously changed hands.

Being spoon-fed and toileted were familiar humiliations, but there was something new: they wouldn't let him sleep. Whenever his head would start to loll, the butt of a rifle would descend on his toes or his instep, sometimes even on his fingers. Keeping him awake was something they did with great enthusiasm. Perhaps they were following orders, but he suspected it was simply sport.

He knew the journey was over when the plane lurched to a halt and his minders burst into patriotic song, keeping time on his head with a roll of papers. When the singing was done, he signed and initialed the papers blindly, wherever they placed his hand. Then they undid the chains and dragged him to the bottom of the ramp, where they made a ceremony of removing the hood and blindfold.

Even with his eyes shut tight, the brightness was overwhelming. He was forced to his knees and made to kiss the tarmac while they posed, one by one, for pictures. After that, they freed his hands and walked him to the terminal through a haze of atomized fuel and dust.

They hired a cab to drive him downtown, strapping him into the backseat as if he were a child. He was given an envelope and told he was officially a free man. One of them reached in, slapped him playfully on the cheek, and warned him not to misbehave. Then the cab pulled away and he was on his own.

He was curious about what had changed in the capital, but not overly curious. This wasn't his city anymore. What mattered was that the cab was warm and no one was there to hurt him. He was asleep before they reached the airport gates.

The cabbie drove until the money ran out, then helped his uncomplaining passenger onto a park bench with pale blue slats. He'd never seen anything like those slats, which had shallow whorls like fingerprints. Even though the whorls were identical from slat to slat, he liked that the bench had them. His own fingerprints were long gone, casualties of a plumber's torch.

The bench was restful. It didn't occur to him to get up and move. He was waiting for someone to tell him what to do.

Commuters began to fill the park. He'd forgotten what his

own people looked like, how they flowed like milk on the foot-paths. Their flesh was firm, their teeth correct and bright.

And such wealth! A dowry on every wrist. Some of them talked into their jewelry; others merely addressed the air in front of their faces. Had they always been so talkative?

The things they carried still served a first purpose. A news-paper was for reading, not fire-starting. A tote bag was for dry things, not game birds, slick with blood.

They strove. No one strove in the marshes, in that mind-emptying heat. Civilization may have started in hot places, but it ended up here, where there was winter, where ice crystals skew-ered the eggs of dormant pests.

He worried about being recognized, but no one really no-ticed him. He supposed he understood. Sunlight seemed to pour right through him. There was very little left of himself.

Eventually he let himself be swept along by rush-hour crowds. Young men in suits barreled past him. Their raw ambition was magnetic. How he wished to be a midge on the eyelid of one of those serious young men, drinking from an optimistic eye! He'd been a serious young man once, a believer. He'd yoked himself. Now he was unyoked.

He wasn't simply drifting, although that's surely what it looked like, the random wanderings of an old derelict. Perhaps there was an element of randomness to his path, but he moved toward certain people, just as he shied away from others. He fol-lowed a sad young woman with a bruise on her neck; he retreated from a police officer with bristling hair. His path was not straight. Like a starfish that can't fight the tide, but nevertheless swims as best it can toward the next meal, he was swimming, too.

He walked for a long time. Eventually he came to rest on the plinth of a huge bronze sculpture. The sculpture was abstract, but the plaque read THE TRIUMPH OF GENERAL CURTIS. A tribute to his famous general. He said the name out loud, once, twice, conjuring the pale, lifeless face. Then he pressed his cheek to cool granite and fell asleep thinking of wartime.

A security guard woke him. It was morning again. His pockets had been gone through. The envelope was missing. He asked the guard whether it made sense to file a report.

The guard laughed, then prodded him with the tip of a polished boot.

Time stretched before him like an empty waterway. He decided to visit certain touchstones, places that had mattered to him or to his parents. Sometimes he couldn't remember which was which. For instance, seeking a particular diner and finding instead a gleaming office tower with a lobbyful of marble, he felt a pang, but later, drinking the dregs of an abandoned cup of coffee, he realized he'd never seen the missing diner with his own eyes. It had been a place his father talked about.

The tower had a prominent water feature. He hadn't tasted the water, at least not yet. There were public drinking fountains in the capital. The city was still hospitable to that small degree. After all of his time in the marshes, a machine that produced cool potable water on demand was something of a miracle.

Imagine, waxing poetic about the miracle of a water fountain! He could sit for a long time thinking about the ramifications of such a machine.

He feared seeing people he knew from happier times, but still he craved it. They would be old now, whereas the capital was a city of youth. Occasionally, a tour bus full of retirees would come to a halt near him. He'd make out the ghosts of gnarled fingers pointing at him from behind tinted windows: *Look, isn't that him? But no, it can't be. Wasn't he hanged?*

These fleeting identifications made him feel less substantial, not more. Being almost recognized was worse than being recognized outright. People saw a faint similarity to the man from those old headlines; therefore he was not that notorious man. Therefore he was no one.

He understood their confusion. He looked different now. He'd lost hair to the prison diet, something he predicted at the beginning. He actually said as much to the prison doctor. *Food like this will make me lose my hair.* The doctor had smiled indulgently and said, *Perhaps you're right. But you should have thought of that before.*

Prison hadn't erased his youthful vanity completely. He'd been a handsome man once. Women had told him that, and it was still with him.

Shopgirls on their lunch break offered him bits of food as if he were a bird. A large stinking bird, but still one of God's creatures, nevertheless a life to be cherished. They were too skinny, these shopgirls. They seemed to hold it as an immutable law not to finish their lunch. Food was to be suffered briefly and then scattered to the animals: the pigeons and squirrels and the toothless old fellow in the park whose courtly manners were so comically at odds with his dereliction. He never rushed to take it, no matter how ravenous he might be. There were rules, even for the fallen. This was the capital!

Sometimes they left him a pastry. How he loved the buttery layers, the texture of sugar crystals on his tongue. One bite, and he was back in his childhood bakery, his mother holding a cookie hostage for a kiss on the cheek. His father standing apart, disapproving. Boys were supposed to be outside playing, not crowding their mother's knees under a café table, clutching a stuffed crocodile. Or perhaps not a crocodile, maybe a snake, some creature from the marshes. This was long before he'd even heard of the marshes, but already its monsters dominated his imagination.

A neighbor's Pomeranian had gotten hold of that stuffed animal and chewed its tail. A great disaster. *There's no need to cry*, his mother had said, *you can fix it with those healing paws of yours.*

2

In good weather, he wandered the Mall, where the hollowed-out eyes of founding fathers seemed to offer a silent reprieve. Everything was just so on the Mall, down to the shadows that crept obediently across warlike friezes. The dazzling marble facades erased differences, silhouetting tourist and bureaucrat alike, unifying everyone in a grand tableau. There was even a place for him; he stood as a warning, an example of what befalls a man unprotected by empire.

On the weekends, crowds would gather on the wide gravel paths opposite the museums. A march, a protest, a rally—it didn't make much difference. Where there was a crowd, there were students; where there were students, there was spare change and food.

Not all of the students were generous. Some were self-righteous. He'd been one of the self-righteous ones. It was hard to tell which was which, since he rarely made eye contact. Eye contact could be taken as a challenge. He knew that about dogs. In the marshes, looking into a man's eyes was a sign of welcome. He still associated marsh greetings with a sliding sensation above his ears, the feeling of sunglasses being removed.

Crowds meant street vendors. He was not welcome among the vendors, who were often fresh immigrants. Nevertheless, he was drawn to them the way he was drawn to marshmen everywhere, out of a sense of kinship. They weren't bold enough to chase him off, but that didn't stop them from saying shamefully inhospitable things to his face. There was no pity among the vendors. He had every possible advantage, including the most prized: skin of the right color. Yet here he was, sniffing around their carts like a stray.

He knew what they thought of him, but he went to them anyway. There were perks: the smell of roasted meat, a bit of stale flatbread, perhaps some charred orts headed for the bin.

Today there was a protest on the steps of the museum of natural history, something about a new exhibit. A politician was making an impassioned speech. The politician wore a business suit, but waved a cadet's shako.

A crowd of angry men in ill-fitting fatigues clustered at the base of the steps. These were middle-aged men wearing the uniforms of youth. Many of them had long hair. Some were draped in regimental colors. Others waved placards that read WE BLED FOR THIS? and HONOR OUR FALLEN, NOT THE ENEMY!

Across the avenue, in front of a stand of towering walnut trees, there was a large counter-protest. These were mostly students. Their contorted mouths were like pretty pink blossoms. They were chanting, "We broke it, we bought it!"

If only he could harvest the energy these young people poured into the air. He wanted to lift up his arms and say, *Relax, children, this is a land of plenty.*

A group of boys broke off from the seething mass and hurled green walnuts at the veterans on the steps. There were cries of outrage. The veterans scattered, collected the nuts, and hurled them back.

It was in this counter-volley that he was struck in the face. One moment he was staring dreamily at the melee; the next, he was on the ground. He couldn't be sure exactly where the nut had struck. His face was numb. He knew he'd been hit, though. His lips were wet with blood.

He was suddenly very thirsty. Just before he fell, he'd been considering the water fountain in the rotunda. It was near the entrance, but had the disadvantage of being one of those low fixtures designed for schoolchildren. He didn't like drinking from it. His hands were unclean. He worried for the children who drank after him.

At any rate, now he was lying on the gravel with protesters all around, some of them quietly conferring, others squatting nearby as if they felt they ought to help, but couldn't quite overcome their disgust.

He didn't blame them for not wanting to touch him. There was no telling what vermin pulsed in his clothes, what virus polluted his blood.

A nervous little marshman in a tracksuit, one of the sausage vendors, parted the crowd. He kept saying, "Excuse me," but his tone implied that anyone standing in his way was either an idler or a fool. He had a woman in tow, a museum worker with a laminated badge. Her stride was confident, but she held herself aloof, wrapping a wool shawl ever tighter around her shoulders.

She thanked the marshman, then turned to the young protesters and said, "We need to move this man. Gently, now." Her words seemed to wake them up. They pressed his arms and legs in encouragement. Someone cried out, "He's going to be okay!" There were murmurs of relief.

They lifted him by his scavenged raincoat and carried him to the side entrance of the museum. Along the way, several of his bearers melted back into the crowd. Now there were only three resentful young men who realized too late that their colleagues had slipped away. They were rough with him, not out of anger, but because their arms were tiring. As they passed through the bronze doors, his mouth brushed the bare arm of one of the young men, who recoiled and cursed.

They laid him on an upholstered bench under the disapproving eye of an elderly guard. The bench sighed, its leather exhaling an odor of wealth. For the first time, he had a good look at the woman who'd intervened on his behalf. She was middle-aged, with dark, tightly curled hair, shot through with white. Her eyes were deep brown and soulful, but diminished by octagonal glasses, bits of burnished gold and plastic that should have lightened her face, but instead gave it a kind of severity.

She wore a gray suit that was well made but old-fashioned, like something she'd found in her grandmother's closet and mockingly tried on, only to discover that it fit quite well—well enough, anyway, to save the expense of buying something new.

She didn't wear makeup. In fact, she looked like someone who thought makeup was silly, but was nevertheless vulnerable to the attention of glamorous department store saleswomen. He wanted to tell her she was right not to wear it, that no one should hide such beautiful tawny skin.

It had been a long time since he'd studied a woman's face so closely. He was surprised to be drawing conclusions from it. That was a skill from his old life, when subtleties mattered, before all he needed to know was whether or not a person meant him harm.

She dismissed the last young man who'd carried him in. The others had already disappeared through the massive revolving door.

She asked if he was comfortable, then offered him an oat bar, rummaging for it in her purse.

He wished she had something else. He avoided food that made him thirsty. This was a city of pay toilets. A homeless man was forced to do his business out in the open, in precisely the way that invited beatings and even arrest.

"Here," she said. "I know it's not great."

He was in no position to refuse it, but he told her that oat bars didn't agree with him, all the while hinting that the problem lay in his teeth. Actually, he had strategies for eating anything, even beef jerky. He knew how to keep food in his cheek until it softened. If that didn't work, there were other ways to break it down.

She slid the bar back into her purse and said she didn't really like them, either, which was why she carried one for emergencies. She wasn't likely to eat an oat bar unless she was truly desperate.

The guard came over and whispered something that made her angry. She walked back to his station, dealing with him sharply along the way, and returned with a guest badge. She made a show of pinning the badge to his chest, then helped him to his feet and led him to an unmarked door, which she opened with a swipe of a security card.

They walked long hallways lined with specimen cases. When he paused to rest in front of one of the cases, a bird with iridescent feathers caught his eye. A male marsh coot. He knew it well. The taxidermist had captured the coot's enigmatic smile, but the eyes were the wrong color; he remembered them as red, not purple.

She explained, as if he were a visiting colleague, that museums were in a time of transition. Merely displaying the wonders of nature was no longer enough. What curators emphasized now was not so much this or that specimen, but rather the story of the scientist or explorer who collected it.

He didn't really understand what she meant but nodded sagely to keep her talking. The businesslike tone of her voice made him feel safe.

Then she told him they were headed to the infirmary, which surprised him. He wondered why there should be an infirmary in a museum.

"There've been accidents," she said. "That's what we're calling them, anyway. Some quite serious." She went on to say that the museum had added extra security, and that its insurer had insisted on a medical station until the new exhibit was finished and all the fuss about it died down. Everyone called it the "infirmary" because the phrase "medical station" seemed awfully heavy. Didn't he agree?

He nodded, but once again, she was talking beyond him. "Medical station" seemed perfectly normal. Had words truly become light or heavy while he was away?

"Here we are," she said, stopping at the open door of an office suite. A male nurse rose from a swivel chair to greet them. He'd been interrupted while reading. He set aside his book and let his reading glasses dangle from a cord around his neck. He was a compact, balding man whose large ears and rosy cheeks nevertheless gave an impression of youth.

She greeted him with a familiarity that aspired to a kiss but didn't quite reach it. There was an uncomfortable spark between them—or perhaps that was just his overactive imagination. Then again, why shouldn't they be a couple? She was lonely. He didn't need all of his wits to see that. Of course there was always the possibility that the nurse was a homosexual, that antique stereotype.

Homosexuality was in vogue in the capital. He'd noticed a surprising amount of public affection between men at rallies on the Mall. The hand-holding might have been tactical, a mirror image of the battle lines of the police, who linked arms when facing a crowd. But he'd seen men holding hands when there were no threatening police to be found.

It didn't really faze him. He'd always envied the easy camaraderie that marshmen shared, which wasn't entirely chaste. A marshman never knew when he might be called to defend his fellow tribesman in a blood feud. He might hold that very tribesman, bleeding to death, in his arms. A precedent of intimacy might prove helpful, even if it was years in the past and forbidden to remember, much less invoke, in those ultimate moments.

The employee lounge had been converted into an examination room. It was strange to undress in front of a vending machine, to warm his bare legs by the coils of a miniature refrigerator. The nurse helped him change into a gown of dimpled crepe, carefully folding his filthy rags and setting them on a side chair, but not before lining the upholstery with table paper.

There had been advances in medical supplies. The gown's soft fabric was one of them, as were the tools the nurse used during his examination, which were sculptural, the steel curving and glistening as if it were still liquid. These were finer tools than he'd ever had in the field. He marveled that a temporary infirmary should be so well stocked.

The nurse proceeded methodically, examining the facial wound first of all, cleaning with disinfectant and probing with tweezers so fine they looked as though they terminated in two metal hairs. As he worked, he applied a balm that instantly made the area numb.

With the numbness came guilt. He'd trained himself to ignore pain for as long as possible, and then, when it could no longer be ignored, to think of it as retribution, a reminder of the pain he'd inflicted on others.

The nurse continued the examination downward, swabbing old wounds as he went, bandaging some, applying his wonderful balm. When the examination was over, and the street grime had been lifted away, the small trash can by the door overflowed with filthy cotton. The nurse then cut his toenails, which were gnarled and yellow, an old man's claws.

He hadn't found a blade sharp enough to cut them, not even the broken penknife he'd tried to whet on a curb with unusually creamy concrete. He'd gouged one of his toes with its jagged steel tip. The wound had festered and was only just beginning to heal.

The nurse made short work of the nails, then handed him an emery board, out of deference to his masculinity. But his fingers were too clumsy to hold the file at the proper angle, and his body was stiff from the fall, so in the end the nurse took back the emery

board. It was a blow to his pride, but what blow hadn't he weathered? He held himself still, closed his eyes, and listened to the
wisp wisp of the file, the tiny pulses of another person attending
to him.

In that peaceful attitude, he drifted off to sleep.

3

He awoke alone in the room. The lights had been dimmed, and there was a heavy packing blanket on his legs. He was still wearing the gown, although he'd torn it in his sleep.

He went to the sink and splashed his face with warm water again and again, then drank with a cupped hand. He reached for his clothes, but they were gone. He didn't blame the nurse for getting rid of them. They belonged in an incinerator.

New clothes had been laid out for him: a janitor's uniform and a pair of briefs still sealed in their retail package. He recognized the name on the label, a fancy downtown haberdashery. The price on the tag was shocking. He hadn't spent much more on his first set of dress whites.

He dressed, leaning heavily against the examining table. The thin blue pants, tied at the waist with a ribbon, reminded him of surgical scrubs, the uniform of his youth. He wondered what surgeons wore these days, whether there was even such a thing as surgery anymore.

The nurse brought him a disposable shaving kit. Before handing it over, he contemplated the safety razor with raised eyebrows, as if to stress that by passing a razor he was breaking an important rule.

He soaked a washcloth in hot water and pressed it to his face. Then he shaved twice, bearing down on the razor the second time, scraping everything away.

When he was done, he realized that he'd gotten blood on the washcloth. He didn't know what to do with it, so he left it in the sink. Other people had cleaned up for him his entire life, in locker rooms and officers' clubs—even in prison. The blood-flecked cloth looked wrong there, but he didn't dare throw it away.

His rescuer had returned and was arguing with the nurse behind the closed door. They were talking too heatedly for mere colleagues. She was telling him it would just be for a night or two. He was saying it was impossible. More than impossible. There was the safety of his family to consider.

She reacted strongly to the word "family." She said she'd done plenty of things for him that his wife hadn't. At that, he lowered his voice and asked her to lower hers. Instead, she issued an ultimatum. The nurse was silent. After a long pause, she said, "I guess that's that."

When she flung open the door to the examining room, he shielded his eyes, fearing she'd recognize him. There'd been a very famous photograph of his eyes on the cover of a magazine. They were duller now, but otherwise unchanged.

She looked him up and down, nodding with approval, and said, "Much better."

She asked if he was ready to go but didn't wait for an answer before taking his elbow. On the way out, he stopped to thank the nurse. After all, the man had seen to his wounds and clipped his grotesque nails, all to earn the rebuke of this hardheaded woman. He tipped an invisible hat, holding it by its imaginary brim.

It was a gesture from another time. He hardly expected the nurse to understand it, but he did. The nurse tipped his own pretend hat.

It brought tears to his eyes.

The nurse's silent farewell followed him down the long echoing halls and out onto the museum's shallow steps.

She helped him down the steps, but when they reached the sidewalk, she didn't relinquish his arm. She guided him to a vendor and bought him a hot chocolate, most likely to spare any back-and-forth over whether he took sugar and cream with coffee. She handed it to him wrapped in a napkin, warning that it was likely to be very hot. He took it gingerly, blowing on it like a child, just to please her.

They waited for a bus. The bus stop was crowded with irritated workers, their manners holding them in check, but just barely. She surveyed the restless crowd and said under her breath that they'd never get home this way. She used her shoulder to make a passageway, leading him to open sidewalk.

They crossed one of the great avenues, eight lanes wide. The janitor's uniform offered little protection from the evening breeze. She saw that he was chilled and stopped to wrap her shawl around his shoulders, right there in the middle of the street. She explained that the streets had been cordoned off for a parade, but just as she said that, a police car raced by and activated its claxon. The sound convulsed his heart like the bare wires they used to touch him with in prison.

"No, you're right," she said, "this can wait until we're on the other side."

She led him through a memorial park. The park was as good a place as any to resume his time alone. He slowed as they passed a familiar steam grate. He might be able to snatch an hour or two of sleep before the police moved him along. Of course, there was a downside to steam. It made one sweat. To be rousted sweating on a cold night was to invite hypothermia.

She slid an arm around him and told him they didn't have far to go. She was very strong underneath all those sensible clothes. When they got to the edge of a busy street, her arm tightened around his ribs, which were still sore from being kicked a few nights before. He hadn't seen his attackers. He'd learned to curl into a ball and howl like a dog the moment he felt the first blow.

He let himself be led under her protective wing. She held

him with one arm and signaled the oncoming traffic with the other, waving two fingers up and down in a tight arc.

A cab detached itself from the blur of vehicles and came to a stop in front of them. She helped him in, then climbed in next to him and shut the door.

The driver didn't want to go where she told him to, but she ignored his objections. She said she was within her rights to be taken where she wanted.

When the cab leaped forward and swerved into traffic, her body pressed against his. He liked how solid she was, even if it squeezed the air from his lungs. Her thigh alongside his was warm and smelled of perfume.

Despite the violent ride, she managed to locate the mating pieces of his seat belt and strap him in. It bothered him to be the more protected one. He reached over to help with her belt, but she patted his hand, then planted it firmly on his lap. The message was clear: it wasn't for him to strap her in.

He closed his eyes, but the car's suspension was loose, and he began to feel a little sick. He could tell from the ripping sound of the tires that they were crossing a long bridge.

He hadn't been to the other side of the river since high school, on a dare. Only factory workers and domestics lived across the river. One didn't cross over unless it was to do some unpleasant business. At least, that was what they'd said back in the day.

Wealth had changed things. They drove past pristine row houses with neatly painted trim. Antique streetlights had been retrofitted with artificial flames.

The streets were freshly cobbled. Corner drugstores had been converted into tony restaurants, their vintage neon signs advertising patent drugs that hadn't been sold for decades.

The sidewalks were crowded with smart young couples pushing strollers. The number of dark faces in the strollers surprised him: babies adopted from the marshes. The homeland birthrate had fallen off while he was in prison. It didn't take an epidemiologist to see that, merely a few weeks drifting through empty playgrounds.

Eventually they reached the edge of the gentrification. The road changed from cobbles to ordinary asphalt. The streetlights were ordinary, too, fitted with harsh sodium bulbs. There were no flowering trees, just buckled sidewalks littered with broken glass. Most of the row houses were boarded up. The driver kept using the word "mudmen": how they lived like rats, how they turned everything into a fucking sewer.

As they drove under an old railroad bridge, rocks rained down on them. The driver cursed, accelerated into a U-turn, and then, at the first opportunity, skidded to a stop and ordered his passengers out.

She argued that it was illegal for him to discharge them this way, but the driver was having none of it. He answered by applying a fat knuckle to the cracked windshield.

She handed him a large bill and asked for change, but he rolled up his window and rocketed away.

Then they were alone on the street. Their path took them back under the railroad bridge. He was an easy target for bad boys. He was frightened, but she kept up a lighthearted chatter about her work at the museum. The clack of her shoes on the sidewalk was steady as a metronome.

Once or twice he caught her looking at him with a sudden intensity, as if to catch him in the act of hearing or not hearing. He tried to pay more attention to what she was saying, but her words battered his ears like moths. There was no capturing them.

She led him to the armored door of a factory building and surprised him by unlocking it with an ordinary key. She explained that the building was a warehouse that had been converted into apartments. She didn't use the word "apartments." She used a new word. He didn't want to sound outdated, so he acted as if he'd heard of such things.

The elevator was cavernous. As its hidden cables roared to life, she seemed suddenly aware of the fact that she was leading a stranger to her door. A certain space opened up between them. He didn't really know how to reassure her. Perhaps he owed it to her, but he didn't bother trying. The new distance came as a relief.

Her hallway was full of cooking smells: seared goat, boiling rice, something floral, perhaps saffron. Marsh cooking. This was a source of great wonder to him. Apparently citizens of the capital now made their homes side by side with marshmen.

When they came to her door, she told him there'd recently been a large levy for roof work, something to do with the high price of copper flashing, which was so very expensive on account of the pointless wars abroad.

Then she swung the door open and held it, inspecting him as he passed, like a teacher on the first day of school.

4

She unbuttoned her jacket in the front hall and dropped it on a rough wooden bench. It bothered him to see such a fine jacket treated that way, but he kept his mouth shut. Why should he care more for her clothes than she did?

She showed him the bathroom. He went in obediently and ran the water for a while, first warm and then hot, holding his hands under the flow, his whole body vibrating with pleasure.

Rather than wipe his hands on a towel, he dried them with toilet paper. He started squirreling some away for later, but it occurred to him that stealing toilet paper was no way to reward her hospitality. He tried to roll it back up, only to find that he'd ruined the sheets with his wet fingertips. He stuffed the ruined paper in the wicker trash basket, staring at it with regret.

He waited in the hallway, listening to the banging of pots, the rapid click of a gas igniter, until she called for him. Then he stood in the kitchen and watched her uncork a bottle of wine.

She filled two glasses, proposing a toast to better times, then set a plate of flatbread in front of him and encouraged him to eat. The bread was tough. He would have liked a bowl of warm milk to soften it, but she was very busy, so he dipped it in his wine instead. The flavors were bad together. When she saw the expression on his face, she laughed and took away the bread, saying there were better things to come.

He was still mourning the loss of the bread when she put out a plate of farmer's cheese and crackers. There was still cheese left after he gobbled all the crackers. He held back for a while, quivering like a faithful dog, but in the end, he ate it all. It took all of his willpower not to lick the plate clean.

The main course was roast chicken and rice. They didn't speak much during the meal. Every few minutes, she served him more rice. The rice was very salty; he washed it down with glass after glass of water. Drinking freely was as great a luxury as the rich food.

When she stood to pour him more wine, her napkin came untucked and fluttered to the floor. Dizziness overcame him as he reached down. His chair tilted forward. Someone seemed to dump him out of it.

He came to on the floor, his cheek resting on the napkin, which smelled of her lap. The scent of her body agitated and comforted him in equal measure.

He offered to do the dishes, but she helped him to the couch and covered him with a throw, saying there was plenty of time for that later.

Closing his eyes, he again thought of himself as a dog, peaceful in his soft-sided crate, his belly full, yet with a nagging sense that he ought to be throwing himself at his master's feet.

The quality of the light changed from time to time. His arms fell asleep, requiring him to roll to different positions. His neck developed a crick.

Then it was morning and she was padding through the room in a thick dressing gown. She turned on all the lights and went to work in the kitchen. The radio came on. A few minutes later, she made it louder.

He sat up and rubbed his eyes. Nighttime twisting had torn open his fly. It hadn't happened for a long time, but he'd woken with an erection. He waited for it to subside, but it was stubborn. When she came to tell him to get a move on, he covered himself with the throw.

She saw, but didn't turn away. Instead, blushing deeply, she looked him in the eye and held her gaze there. The crimson highlighted her lovely skin.

"Wait here," she said, appearing a few minutes later in a long plaid skirt and a blouse that strained a bit at the buttons. She made her hair into a loose bun, pinned it with a pencil, then stepped out.

She returned with an armful of clothes, which she laid out on the coffee table. She said her only neighbor with any spare men's clothing was the widow of a marshman.

He ran his fingers across the handmade garments, which he recognized not only by region, but by tribe. He murmured the name of the tribe to himself and selected a finely woven tunic. It was a very beautiful example of the type. The matching leggings were unusually soft. He didn't recognize the wool.

She took his interest in the leggings as a kind of criticism. "Well," she said, "it's the best I can do," then left him to finish dressing.

It had been a long time since he'd worn marsh dress. He remembered watching elders wrap their leggings with little grunts of painful resignation. Now he grunted, too, as he wound the fragrant cloth.

The tunic fit perfectly. He'd forgotten how good he felt in a tunic and leggings, how free, how ready for action.

She came out of the bedroom fussing with a necklace, a hair clip dangling from her lips like a cigarette. She was surprised that he was already dressed. She studied him with a knowing look that frightened him. He moved away from the coffee table to have a clearer path to the door.

She asked for help with her necklace, and while he fastened it with trembling fingers, she told him he looked very dashing. The way she kept sneaking glances at him eventually melted his suspicion. She was merely pleased with how he looked. He was pleased, too.

They drank orange juice and had a few sips of scalding coffee. She said she didn't really eat in the morning, the implication being that neither would he. He thanked her anyway and told her he was grateful.

She put the cups in the sink and herded him to the door. He didn't really mind being rushed. It gave him energy. All of it was so normal to her and so alien to him, but the gap was closing a bit.

As she locked the door behind them he thanked her again, very quietly this time, using the marsh tongue in order to spare her any embarrassment.

She accepted his thanks with an old proverb: *Hospitality is its own reward.*

Her accent was flawless. He praised her for it, hoping for an explanation, but she acted as if nothing out of the ordinary had passed between them.

A cab was idling out front. "That's for us," she said, tapping his shoulder as if he were hard of hearing, "but don't get used to it."

There was already a long line of tourists at the museum's main entrance, but she whisked him through a temporary door marked EMPLOYEES ONLY, then down a labyrinthine plywood tunnel.

They emerged in a new wing with a swooping glass roof. The morning was overcast, but even so, the glare from the polished floor was severe. He closed his eyes and let a soft wooden handrail be his guide.

The rail ended at a pair of enormous bronze doors with bas-relief panels the size of atlases. The designs were geometric and stylized, but there were certain motifs: reed huts; busy waterways; earthen levees. A sun cast brazen rays across the landscape. The center panel depicted a chief's canoe, its high curving prow echoed by the graceful neck of a stalking ibis.

"I have a meeting," she said. Passing through the doors seemed to make her forget all about him.

He didn't know whether he was supposed to wait or follow her into the exhibition hall, which was even brighter than the hallway. The brightness forced the eyes down, just like in the marshes, and the cleverly painted walls erased any sense of enclosure. The vast scale of the hall—as large as a warehouse, perhaps even larger—was intimidating. There might be anything inside.

The sounds were what finally drew him in: the bellow of water buffalo; the staccato snap of a merganser trying to distract a predator from her ducklings; the dissonance of wind in the reeds.

Somewhere in the distance, a merchant called out his wares: sugar, coffee, steel sewing needles.

He could hear the faint plash of paddles, the gurgle of surface-feeding fish, even the whine of mosquitoes.

There was something else familiar, a quality of light and sound that was very precise: the feeling of a morning after a great windstorm. He remembered those fragile mornings. There was a rawness in the air, a wounded quiet. Earth and sky seemed childishly reluctant to heal.

The verisimilitude was uncanny. He wondered about the curator who'd perhaps said about the lighting, "I like how the shadows purple in the recesses of the buffalo stall, but the sunlight is too sharp for rainy season."

The center of the exhibit was a floating island, the kind heaped up by succeeding generations of marshmen, a hillock of floating grass linked to shore by a swaying rope bridge; and on the island, a proper marsh village, each hut built of painstakingly baled reeds.

The encircling water was artificial, obviously. One couldn't have museum-goers falling into water. But somehow they'd managed to make it just as shimmering and elusive as any waterway in the marshes, its surface bulging, from time to time, with the lips of simulated catfish.

He wanted to kneel down and touch the artificial water, to study its astonishing craftsmanship, but the construction of the grass mound was so authentic that the closer to the shining black shoreline he came, the swampier and less stable was the ground under his feet, until he couldn't move forward for fear of being pitched against the nearly invisible glass guardrail.

He drew back from the edge and moved to higher ground, then crossed the rope bridge and wandered among the huts. In the distance, real or painted, was the distinctive cone of a village kiln, which towered over a yard stacked high with empty brick molds.

Between the reed island and the brickyard, there was a broad wetland, rutted with natural and man-made channels. A camouflaged walkway overhung it.

A meeting was taking place on the walkway. He recognized his friend by the long plaid skirt, so incongruous among the reeds. There were two others: a tall man in a business suit whose yellow hard hat was stenciled with the word DIRECTOR; and a carefully coiffed woman in a brilliant blue dress who knew how to use her body when arguing a point in front of a man.

The director's hands were spread aggressively on his hips. The matter, whatever it was, seemed to have been long settled, but he was working hard to maintain the appearance of fairness.

The discussion reached a high pitch. The director signaled that he'd heard enough, then issued his verdict.

The woman in the blue dress had trouble containing her glee. This was clearly the culmination of a long campaign. The one with brighter plumage had been victorious. The loser stormed off.

The thought of being alone in the exhibit frightened him, so he went to find her. Somehow he knew the lay of the land. Every cut in the red clay, every berm, was oddly familiar.

He followed the river. They'd captured the peculiar sigh the sandy soil made as the river water ran along it, a very distinct sound like the tearing of kraft paper.

He came to a clearing with beached canoes. The canoes seemed authentic, with their curved prows and the bitter aura of bitumen. He got a splinter verifying that the wood was the right species, the pitch the same thick concoction one could smell bubbling in the vats by the water in the dry season, when boats were repaired.

There was a guesthouse nearby, a tiny cathedral executed in bundled reeds. How he'd wanted a guesthouse of his own! It took many years for him to understand that the reason he couldn't get one built had nothing to do with a shortage of skilled workers, or even with the bad feelings toward the occupation, but rather with the transgressive nature of the desire itself. It was wrong to want a communal building for one's own. No one had taught him that in his own country. That lesson had been left to marshmen.

She was inside the guesthouse by the long rectangular hearth, sobbing and cradling her purse. The rules of the marshes applied even here, in a museum in the capital. He didn't know why, but they did. He was entitled to enter a guesthouse, no matter the emotional state of anyone else. If she'd truly wanted to be left alone, she could have chosen any of the reed huts that dotted the path.

Marshmen would often find their way to a guesthouse when they were suffering the throes of indecision or grief. There was comfort in numbers, even if some of the guests might, on the surface, be strangers. There was always coffee, always a bowl of rice, sometimes fresh, sometimes stale, but nourishment, nonetheless. He'd sought comfort there, too, during the long occupation, but never managed to shed the burden of his uniform.

5

She didn't acknowledge his presence, but it was her right not to. The guesthouse was a public place, but one that nevertheless allowed for a certain amount of privacy.

He lingered by the door, even though he was curious about the hearth, which had been prepared for a demonstration of the coffee ceremony. An authentic kettle hung from an iron tripod. There was a sack of marsh coffee, a grinder, a coffeepot— everything necessary for a hospitable cup, even a battered tin of sugar.

Marshmen started coffee fires the ancient way: with flint. When he was first shown the fire starters, which were shaped like spearheads, he'd marveled at the ingenuity of finding a domestic use for a killing point. Later, he was told that the similarity of the fire starters to spear tips was coincidental, but he preferred to think of it his own way: the beating of a sword into a plowshare. It seemed to represent progress. This was back when he believed in progress, when he saw himself as an agent of it.

The fire starters were supposed to be in a leather bag that hung from a hook as one entered the guesthouse, always on the right, never on the left. He looked on the right side, but there was no leather bag. Neither was it on the other side of the doorway.

In addition to the fire-starting fetish about left and right, the marshmen also had a rule about north and south. He walked the length of the guesthouse and found the bag hanging in exactly the wrong place: by the left side of the southern door.

He took the bag and hefted it. Its precious shifting contents felt strangely intimate in his palm. He looked around self-consciously, but there was no one here to call him out, no one to mock him.

He squatted by the hearth and made a small pile of dried grass. He could sense objections forming inside of her, but she didn't voice them. The tinder pile sparked easily. He built up a mound of sand around the base of the tripod, and as the water heated in the kettle, he added a ring of stones. The stones weren't really necessary. There was plenty of sand to kill a fire, but he wanted her to relax.

He toasted a handful of coffee beans, then ground them. The grinder was fancier than he was used to. It had a porcelain knob. He was used to wooden knobs worn smooth by palm leather. He tapped the grounds into two empty cups.

Her interest was gathering, along with the impulse to tell him to put these things down. These were artifacts, museum property. Who was he to handle them? But she saw that he knew what he was doing. It had been decades since he'd made marsh coffee, but it all came easily back.

When it was time to pour from the kettle, he wrapped his sleeve around the hot wire handle. Only then did he realize he'd made a mistake: marshmen never brewed coffee by the cup. They brewed it in a tall coffeepot with a long wooden handle; a fine example was sitting practically under his nose. How had he forgotten that crucial step? It had all seemed so natural up to that point.

He ransacked his memory for a time—a bivouac or hunting trip—when he'd seen coffee brewed by the cup.

Once begun, the ritual must not be interrupted. Part of the pleasure of the marshman's coffee was its preparation, which followed along scrupulous lines. He rinsed the coffeepot and then decanted the foaming cups into it, declaring with this gesture that he'd meant to make two cups of coffee and two cups only, rather than an entire pot. Of course, in the marshes, such precision would have been interpreted not only as frugal, but also as downright rude.

There was a certain showmanship involved in pouring coffee from a height. He'd known experts who could extend the stream nearly a yard without spilling a drop. He raised the pot as much as he dared with his unsteady hands.

He was glad to find the sugar in its authentic state, too, fused in small chunks like gemstones. He gave her one and took one for himself. A marshman liked to hold the sugar in his front teeth while he drank.

She started to drink that way, then shifted the sugar to her cheek. This was an expression of her good manners. She didn't want to make him feel self-conscious.

In that way, she was unlike a woman of the marshes, who would have been glad for the chance to demonstrate the superiority of her teeth.

They sat in silence and sipped their coffee, listening to the distant lowing of water buffalo. As faithful as the recordings were, they'd been produced with the average length of a museum-goer's visit in mind. The sounds cycled every few minutes. The same water buffalo was ever lowing, the same waterfowl criss-crossing the sky.

He waited for her to speak. It was pleasant to be sitting in a guesthouse, in the proper clothing, sipping sludgy coffee. He'd always felt at home in the marshes. That comfort had been at the very heart of his troubles.

Finally he broke the silence, saying that he was certainly no expert, but he did wonder whether the fire starters were in their proper place.

"I know!" she said, adding that she'd pointed it out herself, but was overruled by one of her colleagues who produced a photograph to bolster his claim. Her theory was that the photograph had been printed backward, an occupational hazard with old negatives.

The subject ran its course. There was another lull, which he finally ended by saying the exhibit was brilliant. He didn't mean to sound patronizing, but praising her efforts, dressed as he was, in that setting, was practically the definition of the word. He was an elder. In the guesthouse, offering praise or criticism wasn't just permitted; it was his essential role.

She started to cry. He didn't try to soothe her. He simply made himself still until the crying stopped. She thanked him and went on to say that she'd just been handed a tough decision. A terrible insult, really.

He made more coffee the same way as before, which caused her to tell him, very gently, that she'd never seen it done that way.

He laughed and said he knew it was wrong, but hadn't wanted to admit it.

She took two sugars. She'd wanted two sugars before, she said, but was ashamed of her sweet tooth. Then she told him that some very powerful politicians had threatened to block the museum's funding on account of the marsh exhibit. They claimed it was too "neutral," meaning that the marshman was nowhere held responsible for his crimes against the homeland. Nowhere was there mention of the bloody insurgency that had cost so many lives, or of the barbaric practices that were routinely employed against coalition forces.

She smiled ironically. "And all we did was drain the marshes and destroy their civilization."

The director had given in to the politicians. A huge kiosk

devoted to the crimes of the insurgency was to be installed in the middle of the exhibit, destroying the illusion of natural-ism she'd worked so hard to create. All she'd wanted was to re-create a way of life that had vanished, but now the exhibit would be a war memorial. The marshman's guerrilla tactics and methods of torture would be showcased. All the old ste-reotypes were to be studiously reinforced. It was sure to be very popular.

He considered telling her that the kiosk would be balm for the nation's guilt; that war memorials were building blocks of empire; that museums were no different from any other institu-tion: it took money to keep the doors open. But she was too up-set for platitudes. He leaned in to dry her tears with his sleeve. Then, drawn closer by the gravity of her round wet cheeks, he closed his eyes and kissed her.

After the kiss, she sat quietly for a few moments, then pulled a tissue from her purse and wiped her mouth. She got up, brushed the stiff fabric of her skirt, and walked the length of the guesthouse. When she returned to the hearth, she nodded, and in a voice full of resentment told him she understood.

He didn't really know what she meant. What was there to understand? She'd bared herself to him. He'd seen a bit of him-self reflected there and reached for it, like the boy in the an-cient myth.

He was a broken-down relic. He knew that. She was strong and healthy and so much younger. It was a shameful mismatch. Now he saw just how shameful. Who was he to think he could comfort her?

She said she was running late and asked him to hurry up and finish his coffee.

He put out the cooking fire, and then, in the surest sign yet that she'd ceased to trust him, she knelt down and heaped extra sand on the buried embers, as if to suggest that he didn't know how flammable a reed hut could be.

But of course he knew. He'd seen his share of burning villages.

She didn't look back at him during the long walk to the exit. The lighting was undergoing a test. They were working on sunset. One of the attempts in particular was very much like the way night fell in the marshes, suddenly and completely, like a loss of consciousness.

She stopped at the bronze gates and fumbled with her purse. The sight of it alarmed him. He told her she'd already been far too kind.

"Yes, well," she said, "you may need this." She handed him her business card. The tiny letters swam before his eyes: *Thali Addison*.

She told him to come back at the end of the day. She'd be in meetings all afternoon fighting a holding action.

He found it sad that she used the language of war to describe her workday, and in such a peaceful setting as the back halls of the museum, where even the dust motes seemed to follow the rules of an unspoken truce.

He quit the museum and wandered windblown streets, his lips tingling from the coffee. Towering clouds dominated the sky. The air was raw. His new clothes kept him warm, but he was hungry again. He felt dazed and alone, like a doted-on housecat suddenly forced to live by its wits.

He sat at a playground for a while and watched the clouds. A pair of boisterous twins came to play on the swings, but their parents spirited them away when they saw how he was dressed. He didn't mind. Clouds were easier to watch than children; no one glared at him for looking.

He lost track of time and hurried back to the museum, only to learn by the lobby clock, which was fixed to a stela imported from some conquered desert or other, that he'd been gone for less than an hour. The guards took an active interest when he settled onto one of the leather benches. He considered showing them the business card, but decided not to.

A change had come over him. He was less frightened than before. He took off his shoes and sat cross-legged on the bench, like an elder determined to drink in the peace of the evening before disputants arrived to shatter the calm.

6

After work, they walked side by side against the evening chill. The streets were busy. From time to time, he moved to avoid another pedestrian, but she held him firmly by the arm. She interpreted his desire to pull away as fear. She told him it was natural; everyone feared the dentist.

This was the first he'd heard of their destination. So he was to be a project. What had he been thinking, kissing her like that? He was nothing more to her than a stray. You took strays to a vet, first and foremost, to make sure their health wasn't a threat to your own.

They shuffled awkwardly through the revolving door of an office tower and took the elevator to the twentieth floor. Her dentist was prosperous enough to work high in a downtown building; already his mind was reeling from the debt she was planning to incur on his behalf.

The dentist's office was streamlined and spotless. There were no magazines to clutter the glass coffee table. The only books were a set of pristine historical almanacs that ran the length of a locked credenza.

She filled out some paperwork at the counter, then came and sat next to him on the hard leather sofa, whispering a steady stream he couldn't quite hear. She seemed genuinely happy to be helping him. And why not? She'd arranged a no doubt expensive dentist's appointment for a derelict who sorely needed it. She

had every right to feel good about herself. She looked like someone who felt good about herself too rarely, when by all rights she
should feel it every waking hour.

The dentist was tall and gaunt and wore a yellow bow tie
under his prominent Adam's apple. He had a politician's folksy
manner, but his spit-polished shoes spoke of a man with a history in the service. He gave her hair a playful fluff and said he'd
heard the exhibit was really coming along. Then he winked and
said, "Let's take a look at your new protégé."

His examination involved three quick forays into the mouth,
with a change of gloves each time he made notes with his tor-
toiseshell fountain pen. "Right," he said, turning to announce
that aside from one fairly deep cavity, the remaining teeth were
sound. He waved her off when she asked if the cosmetic work
was going to be terribly involved. "Not to worry," he said. "I'll
put it on your tab."

There were several injections, but he never felt anything worse
than a pinprick. The drill made an eerie breeze on the back of
his tongue.

There had been great advances in dentistry. Or perhaps private dentistry had been different for a long time. No sooner had
the dentist finished filling the cavity than he started rummaging
through a drawer labeled TEETH, INDIVIDUAL AND SMALL GROUP-
INGS. The new teeth were fitted with the help of a wand that cast
gorgeous purple light.

After the final adjustments, the dentist ran a gloved finger
across the repairs, closing his eyes to better concentrate with his
fingertips.

The last step was to polish the teeth to erase any remaining
differences. Only then did he step back to take in the overall
effect.

"Your friend looks awfully familiar," the dentist said.

"He has one of those faces," she said.

"No, I've seen him before. I just can't place him." The dentist excused himself and left the room.

Supine on the armless chair, he suddenly felt very small and exposed. The anesthesia didn't mask the feeling that a great trauma had happened in his mouth. He ran first his tongue, and then a tentative finger, across his new teeth. It felt as though a door that had been left naggingly open was at last closed. But for how long?

The dentist burst back in waving one of the historical almanacs. He handed her the open book, slapping the page with the back of his long elegant fingers. "There, you see?" he said. "It's him."

It was the famous photograph from his trial. He was sitting in the dock, looking small and haunted. The prosecutor was holding up the boy's homemade blade, a miniature marsh dirk. The caption simply read, "Betrayed!"

While she studied the picture, the dentist loomed over him, flexing his jaw. He wished the chair had arms or side rails, anything to cling to. Part of him expected the violence and even welcomed it, but he couldn't manage even the one sit-up that would restore him to the level of the conversation. His stomach muscles were in revolt.

She handed the book back to the dentist. "Yes, I see," she said. Then, without another word, she helped him up from the dentist's chair and led him out, slowing only to leave her card with the receptionist, along with instructions for mailing the bill.

His knees went weak when the elevator doors closed behind him, but she didn't offer a steadying hand. He wanted to tell her that the man in the picture was a different man, which was essentially true, but not factual.

The elevator went up instead of down. She gave a self-mocking laugh. There couldn't have been any more contempt in her voice. He wanted to beg her not to be scornful of her kinder impulses.

The elevator traveled to the top of the building, then descended again, stopping at the dentist's floor. When the doors opened, the dentist himself was standing there in a shearling coat and green fedora. He consulted his watch and stepped into the elevator, turning his back on them as soon as he crossed the grooved threshold.

He announced that he wished to go to the lobby. He was apparently someone who disdained pressing his own elevator buttons. When they were under way, he spoke to her over his shoulder. "No more," he said. "That's the last one."

She held the door for him at the lobby. They stayed in the elevator until his sharp footsteps were gone.

He was prepared to go his own way when they reached the sidewalk. The fresh air was bracing. Sounds from a distant street festival bounced gaily off the glass facades.

"I should have told you," he said.

He tracked the motion of her pupils as they flitted across his face. "I know exactly who you are," she said. "It's a shame you don't know me."

They took a bus that crossed the river on a new suspension bridge with huge green towers. The bus was nearly empty, but she didn't sit beside him; neither did he move to sit beside her.

Eventually she reached up and tugged the signal wire. She called out a word of thanks to the driver, who lifted a weary hand in acknowledgment.

She didn't help him down to the sidewalk, not even when he stumbled. Her pace was quicker than before. She waited impatiently at intersections.

She led him through an overgrown park to the gates of an

armory made of huge granite blocks, along the lines of a fortress from an earlier century. They ducked under a rusting portcullis, then forced their way through a pair of swollen oak doors. There was a security desk, complete with lamp and logbook, but no guard.

The long arched hallways were tiled to shoulder height. The sameness of the cracked white tiles disoriented him. There was a slight tilt to the floor that pushed him ever forward, as though the building were drinking him down. As they walked, the staccato clang of some pump or other grew louder, then softer.

When they came to a locked metal door, she pulled out her overburdened key chain. The lock was sticky. He watched her work the key in and out, wondering how she could possibly be part of such a place.

Beyond the locked door was a vast room, once a workshop of some kind, judging from the axles and flywheels overhead, equipment from a time when everything was driven by a single source of power, a waterwheel or a steam engine. The heavy machinery was long gone, the leather belts and pulleys stripped away. Everything was whitewashed. The center of the room was partitioned with hanging sheets of sandblasted glass.

"There are hospitals in this city that still won't treat marshmen," she said. "The ones that do often require payment in cash. So we've set up a free clinic for them."

She led him to a waiting area full of austere furniture softened with pillows made from tribal rugs. She told him she had to check on something, but that he could rest if he needed to. He sank heavily into a chair.

He had no idea how much time passed before her warm hand touched his neck. His head bent instinctively to it, like a cat to its owner's fingers, but she pulled away. The breaking of that connection was what finally woke him.

He would have been happy to spend the night in that chair, surrounded by the musk of dried marsh grasses, but she took

him to one of the glass-paneled rooms and told him to be prepared to work in the morning.

The room was small but efficient. There was a sink, a set of
drawers, a scale, and an examination table, which she'd made up
as a bed with a blanket and a pillow scrounged from the waiting
area. She told him that the water from the tap was potable, but
she recommended drinking from the glass carboy at the end of
the hall. She looked very tired.

He wanted to apologize and ask how they knew each other;
instead, he thanked her again for her hospitality.

There was no rejoinder this time, no proverb. She closed the
door behind her and paused outside as if trying to decide whether
to lock it. Then her blurred shadow disappeared.

She hadn't shown him a bathroom. He splashed some water
on his face, but didn't drink.

When the lights went out, he pictured her throwing a huge
industrial switch. He approved of her frugality. Even so, he
wished she'd left him with a little light.

He felt his way to the examining table and climbed on. The
blanket was thick and rough and smelled like carbolic. He fell
asleep remembering the harshness of winter in the marshes, and
how he used to listen for spring peepers, whose mating song,
so insistent and piercing, offered the promise of warmer nights
to come.

7

He groaned and covered himself when the lights came on. There was whispering outside the door. He got up, rinsed his mouth, and brushed his teeth with a curved finger. His jaw ached from the dentist, but he took pleasure in his mouth's new solidity.

He needed to find a bathroom. He was hungry, too. He re-wrapped his leggings, smoothed his caftan, and ventured out.

There were orderlies about, weather-beaten women from the marshes who went about their business preparing the examination rooms as if he didn't exist.

A young marshman with unusually dark skin folded a newspaper and rose from one of the wicker chairs. He offered his hand, saying it had been a long time since there was a real doctor in residence. He'd been doing the best he could, but his training was cursory, and really only in the area of emergency response. Sadly, he was all the doctor there was for this underserved population. Also, he added, if anyone overheard a marshman calling him *Doctor*, it was only an honorific. He had no interest in passing himself off in any way above his station.

He asked the marshman to direct him to the restroom.

"Of course," he said, "how thoughtless of me."

The restroom was bright and clean. There was a vase by the sink with fresh flowers, and a stack of worn but neatly ironed hand towels in a grass basket. After washing his hands, he ran the water a while longer, as if he were inspecting the plumbing of a new home.

The marshman was waiting for him just outside the door. "Satisfactory? Good," he said, tucking his newspaper under his arm. "To breakfast, then."

A buffet had been set up in the waiting area. There was warm flatbread, yogurt, and an assortment of fruit—some fresh, some canned, but all of it indigenous to the marshes.

He loaded his plate, cleaned it, and went back for an even larger helping. It was more than he could eat. This was the second instance of waste—the first being the profligate use of water in the restroom—and the day was less than an hour old. It was amazing what was coming back to him, now that he was fed and rested.

Presently the marshman asked if he was ready to start seeing patients. Just as they were about to enter one of the examining rooms, a boy with tiny gray teeth ran up and announced that there was an urgent case with a baby.

"Go on," the marshman said. "I'll join you when I can."

At that, the youngster darted off, shouting for everyone to make way. Perhaps he'd been born in the capital, but his joyful warning was reminiscent of the naked boys who careened through villages announcing strangers. They were obnoxious, those boys, but one forgave them. By sounding the alarm, they were proving their usefulness, and were thus harbingers not just of visitors, but also of their own manhood.

He knocked before entering the room. The mother was sprawled on the examining table, resting her head on an outstretched arm, while the baby soughed quietly in a reed basket on the floor. Her face was uncovered. Her long black hair was pinned up, revealing a graceful neck stippled with goose bumps. Aside from a bruised eye, she was a picture of marsh womanhood. The careless way she flaunted her beauty reminded him of his prettiest tent girl, the one who called herself Betty.

She looked him slowly up and down. She seemed surprised by the color of his skin, but not terribly surprised. She sat up, nodding in the way of someone who knows a thing or two about the world. A new man had come onto the scene, supplanting the old one. She shifted the basket with her foot, drawing it nearer to signal that whatever else might be negotiable, the child was not.

He slung a stethoscope around his neck and picked up a clipboard, hoping that the medical props would bolster his nerves. Then he asked if she was well.

Well enough, she said.

May I examine you?

Her answer was to lean back against the wall and start to lift her dress.

He gently intercepted her wrist to take her pulse.

She shrugged, sat up, and started rocking the basket with the side of her foot.

Her vitals were fine. She didn't want to talk about the bruised eye. She said she was there for her son, who was refusing food, which worried her because he'd always been a regular trencherman.

He made a show of warming the metal part of the stethoscope and testing it on his own forearm, the way he'd seen mothers testing the temperature of baby bottles. The business with the stethoscope relaxed her a bit. Then he asked if he could have a look at the little fellow.

The child was small for his age and very thin. The heart and lungs were healthy, but palpating the swollen belly made him wail.

She said the boy had been breast-fed, but in the last few weeks she'd been weaning him. She mentioned a particular solid food she'd been trying.

When he said he hadn't heard of it, she repeated the name slowly, pantomiming the opening of a small jar. He recognized the characteristic consonant changes that occurred when a marsh-man was trying to pronounce a difficult word in the language of the homeland. He guessed it was a brand of baby food.

When he asked if it came from a store, she shook her head and said she got it from a cousin who sold jars the stores didn't want anymore. She said that breast-feeding was what people did in the marshes. They were in the capital now, where babies ate proper food.

He played with the boy's index finger, which was papery and limp. *Sister*, he said, *do you want your son to be healthy?*

She nodded.

Then listen to him. He's telling you what he thinks of store-bought food.

She nodded again, slower.

Then, in a confidential aside, he told her that his own mother had insisted on breast-feeding him long after other children his age were eating solid food.

Her eyes widened. *Is that true?* she asked.

Actually, it wasn't. His mother had disdained breast-feeding; she'd always referred to it with a wrinkle of the nose as "that procedure." But he felt justified in telling a little lie. It made him angry to think about the money the woman was spending in the name of modernity, while her baby wasted away.

In the next room, a marshman with an oily baseball cap pulled low over his eyes sat on the edge of the examining table, sunk in thought. Before any words could be exchanged, the marsh-man sat bolt upright, staring straight ahead as if this were a military inspection, not a medical one.

The cause for the visit was obvious. His left hand was wadded with stained gauze. The bandage was filthy and held in place with clear packing tape.

He surprised the man by starting his examination not with the wound, but with a few mundane questions. *Are you eating well? Are you having any trouble with your digestion?* And then, leaning in, he asked whether everything was all right in the sack.

This brought a wry grin. The marshman confided that, ever since the accident, he hadn't really had an appetite for women.

He played along, clucking his tongue. He said there'd been a period in his own life, after a fall from a horse, when he couldn't perform his marital duties. His wife had packed her bags and moved to her mother's house for three months.

None of this was true, except for the part about the fall from the horse, which had been quite serious. The marshman perked up at the mention of riding. He asked if the doctor really rode.

Yes, of course, he said, *although not as much as I used to.*

The marshman commiserated. Back home, his uncle had been a horse trader. One of his chores as a youth had been to take his uncle's new horses for a ride in the dunes in order to gauge their desert-worthiness. He remembered riding for hours across trackless sand. Sometimes, if the horse was strong, he'd dig in his spurs, close his eyes, and gallop blind. He said it was like being lifted up in a whirlwind.

You must miss riding very much.

The marshman shook his head. His flight of fancy was over. He said that he worked in a noodle shop. Sometimes the machine that cut the noodles jammed. Clearing jams was part of his job. Someone had turned it on while his hand was involved with the blade. The machine had taken his fingers, but luckily just the tip of his thumb.

Here, he said, hastily unwinding the bandage.

There's no rush.

The marshman smiled mirthlessly. *It's all right*, he said, *there's no pain until the end*. Before tearing off the last of the gauze, he paused for a moment to remove his cap, which was dark with sweat, and set it aside. When he ripped the last of the bandage free, his whole body convulsed. A croak came from his gaping mouth, but he didn't cry out.

The odor of the crusted stumps was nauseating, but the cap was hiding something worse: a ring of scars around the head, like the impression of a thorny crown.

He knew how a marshman got scars like that. He'd watched his own soldiers wrap the razor wire and pull it tight.

He went to the sink and ran the water until the dizziness passed. The mere sound of it was soothing. He splashed some on the back of his neck, then turned to the marshman and apologized. *My heart is old and weak*, he said.

He readied a bowl of warm water and a heap of loose cotton and began to clean the stumps. The crust was stubborn, so he had the marshman soak his hand. He changed the water several times to keep it warm.

When the suturing was finally exposed, he saw that the stitches were tight and regular, the work of a skilled amateur. Ordinary sewing thread had been used. He asked who'd done the stitching. The marshman said he'd done it himself. One of his coworkers had helped—a man, he added pointedly, who didn't faint at the sight of blood.

He ignored the insult and told the marshman he'd done a fine job. The wound was healing well except for one stump that had gotten infected. There was a risk the infection would spread if he didn't do a better job of dressing it.

He salved the stumps with antibiotic ointment and bound them. When he was done, the bandage looked like a boxer's hand-wrapping. It pleased the marshman, although he was loath to show it.

Is it comfortable? he asked. *Did I wrap it well?*

Well enough, the marshman said.

Do you mind if I ask about the scars on your head?

The marshman shrugged. *When they wanted something, your people were very thorough.*

8

There was a surge of patients at lunchtime. It was good to see so many marshmen in one place. He understood a roomful of marshmen in a way he couldn't hope to understand his own people. They were practical above all else. Factory workers who'd spent their lunch hours patiently waiting made way for a child with a painful ear infection. He admired their selflessness. It would have been easy to raise a fuss, or try to slip the doctor a few carefully folded bills.

He saw patient after patient. Most of the cases were straightforward: pink eye, pubic lice, shingles. Treatment was limited to what was on hand in the clinic. Often, the best he could suggest was an herbal remedy.

He'd made quite a study of folk healing in the marshes. There was a lot he could do for the children and elderly, who were open to traditional ways. The middle generation, however, was skeptical. A prescription of herb tea upset them. What did they need him for, if all he had to offer was a remedy they could have gotten from any street peddler?

He tried to explain that the old ways were often the best, but in fact there were plenty of cases beyond his ability to treat. The elegant woman, for instance, with several grandchildren in tow, who presented very serious neck tumors. He sent the children off to play, then waited in silence as she unwrapped her long headscarf. The tumors were advanced. All he could do was give her aspirin to try to ease the pain.

By the end of the day, he was exhausted. Standing in place took a greater toll on his legs than a day of drifting. Being sociable was tiring, too; listening for hours on end, making himself quiet. What he really wanted was to slink back to his room, kick off his shoes, rub his swollen feet for a minute or two, and fall asleep under the rough blanket.

The orderlies were leaving for the night. He heard distant bolts ramming home.

He went to the buffet table, but the food had long been cleared away and the tabletop scoured clean. All of the trash had been taken out. The trash cans in each examining room had been lined with fresh bags. The supply carts had been restocked and were parked neatly in a row.

He collapsed into one of the easy chairs and drank a juice box he'd found in a cabinet, perhaps stashed there to pacify a child. The juice was sickly sweet, but he gulped it down.

He started to drift off but the juice went right through him. The restroom was locked. He had no idea where to begin looking for the key. His need was urgent, so he filched a bedpan from one of the supply carts and took it back to his room.

Just as he was finishing, he heard a faint "Hello?" It was Thali. He tried to hide the bedpan, but she burst in before he found a place for it.

The color was back in her cheeks. Her arms were full of grocery bags. She told him how pleased she was to hear the good report about his work that day. Apparently, he was a big hit with the patients. Perhaps not so much with the orderlies, but they were a famously difficult bunch.

She apologized for being so late, but she'd been held up at work. She'd met with a powerful woman on the museum's board of directors who agreed with her views on the marsh exhibit. With an ally like that, perhaps she stood a chance of reversing the director's decision. At any rate, it had been a long and productive day, and she was in a mood to walk. Would he mind if they walked rather than took the bus?

He nodded and said, "Yes—I mean, no." He'd spent the day talking to marshmen of every stripe; now he was having trouble stringing two words together in his own tongue.

"First things first," she said. She went to a closet and came out with the key to the restroom.

"Here," she said, "I thought you might want to freshen up."

He went to the restroom and emptied the bedpan into a toilet, then leaned against the stall for a few moments and closed his eyes. Water was dripping somewhere, perhaps in one of the huge old porcelain sinks. The way it echoed put him in mind of a cave. He pictured wet formations, spires and stalactites.

It cheered him to think there were slow accretions happening all around.

They left through a gate that overlooked the Mall, with its neat row of brilliantly lit monuments. Their glowing marble filled him with feeling—not patriotism, certainly, but perhaps a cousin of it, a sense of pride in being affiliated with so much power. He turned to her and said, with breath that left traces in the frosty air, that he wanted to give her flowers.

She burst out laughing and kissed his cheek, then gave him one of the lighter bags and hooked her free arm through his. She said there wasn't a florist for miles, when what they both knew she was saying was that he couldn't possibly afford flowers. He told her that she was a formidable woman, a born diplomat. She patted his arm as if he were an unwelcome suitor who'd just made a surprisingly good case for himself.

He was familiar with her neighborhood now. The cavernous elevator in her building no longer seemed threatening. There was no awkwardness at her door. She simply opened it before them,

sat him down on the sofa, and fixed him a drink. He tried to refuse it, but she insisted, saying it was good for his nerves.

The drink was mostly tonic water with a splash of inexpen-
sive gin. He would have preferred whiskey, but took several sips
just to be sociable. It was full of ice and gave him a chill. He told
her that tending bar was yet another of her talents. She answered
from the kitchen that he was a liar, but a sweet one.

He finished the drink in a few long gulps, the faster to be done
with it. His plan was to return the tumbler to the kitchen and
to tell her how good everything smelled, but he couldn't seem to
stand.

The sofa began to swallow him. He felt he was sinking up to
the waist in cool desert sand. The sand around his thighs was
especially cold. It had absorbed the frigid night air and was
releasing it into his bones.

He woke to the sight of her kneeling at his feet, pressing a
towel to the carpet. His empty glass was on the coffee table. There
were ice cubes in his lap.

"You must have dozed off," she said. He picked up an ice cube
and tried to drop it in the glass, but somehow managed to miss.
The cube hit the edge of the coffee table and shattered.

"Please," she said, "don't worry about it. It's just ice. It's just
water."

"I'm a fool," he said.

"No," she said, "it was an accident."

"Stupid, stupid," he said.

"Really," she said, "all I wanted was for you to relax a bit."

He started to cry. His tears were as surprising to him as they
were to her.

"No, no, no," she said, "please."

He apologized, but couldn't stop. "There's a medical term for
this," he said.

"You mean for crying?" she said. "Does it really need one?"

She got up and went back to the kitchen. He heard the banging of pots and pans, followed by a curse. He was awake now. He got down on the carpet, still feeling woozy, and went over the wet area with his sleeve. An ice cube had skittered under the sofa. He tried to reach it, but it was too far away. Still, it felt good to lie down.

When she came back and saw him on the floor, she helped him up, but brusquely. There was irritation in her voice when she announced that dinner was ready. She sat him at the little table in the kitchen facing the sink, which was piled high; it looked as though she'd used every pot and pan in the kitchen to prepare their meal.

She served him in silence. He waited for her to be seated, but she went to the sink and began cleaning up.

He asked her to join him, but she insisted that he go ahead and start.

He was certainly hungry enough. The food smelled delicious. The drink and tiny nap had sharpened his appetite. He still had no idea what she'd prepared. Some kind of meat stew with wild rice.

Finally, she realized he wasn't going to eat without her. She made herself a plate with very small portions and sat down.

There was no talking for a while. The stew was the kind of dish that should have been simmered for hours. Even so, the flavors were good. He liked the rice the best. She made it in the marsh style, sautéing it with a bit of onion before adding water, which made it glutinous. He could have eaten several helpings of the rice with gravy, but there was no way to leave the meat, so he ate the meat as well, cutting it into bits.

She misinterpreted his fastidious cutting. She apologized and said she should have known that his teeth would still be sore.

Even though he didn't want there to be any untruth between them, he was grateful for a reason not to have to eat the meat, which was very strong and gamey. She asked if he knew what kind of meat it was.

He shook his head.

She smiled triumphantly and told him it was wild boar. She obviously considered boar a great delicacy. Here in the capital, it probably was, but back in the marshes he used to hunt boar all the time, not for the meat but to ease the burden of the farmers, whose crops were ravaged by wild pigs, and who were often victims of their deadly attacks.

He started to say something about boars, but she cut him off. "Would you be interested in staying on at the clinic?" she asked.

It was an odd question. She made it sound as though working there had been his idea. He said that being with patients made him feel useful, but he doubted he had much to contribute.

She told him he was being too hard on himself. "It was only your first day," she said. Then she asked him what he thought the clinic needed.

"A real doctor, for a start," he said.

"Seriously, what else?" she said, handing him some paper and a mechanical pencil. "Make a list. Think of it as a village dispensary, a place equipped to handle anything short of major surgery."

The phone rang. She answered it in the living room while he worked on his list. The problem interested him.

He'd already made a page of notes when she came back to the kitchen and leaned on his shoulder. Her eyes were brimming over.

"So much for my ally on the board," she said.

He wrapped an arm around her waist. She curved herself to him and stood that way for a time.

"They're going to ruin my village," she said. "For the second time."

"I'm so sorry," he said.

There were only a few ways for the evening to resolve itself, all of them complicated. He asked if he could use her shower. She told him he was welcome to.

He showered without any thought of how much hot water he was using. The bathroom was full of steam by the time he finished. The towels were all very large. He wrapped himself up to the armpits in one before going back out.

She'd laid out fresh clothes for him on her bed. He took them back to the bathroom and dressed. The bathroom was very small and the floor was wet, but he was glad of a few more minutes behind a closed door.

He found her asleep on the couch in the living room, a half-empty bottle of wine nearby on the coffee table. She was snoring; her parted lips revealed purplish teeth. He tried to help her to bed, but she rolled away from him, so he gave up and covered her with a sofa blanket. Then he sat by her on the floor, from time to time brushing the hair from her sleeping eyes.

His legs fell asleep, and still he didn't move. He found himself humming an old song.

"That's pretty," she said.

"Go back to sleep," he whispered.

"It sounds like a marsh tune," she said, reaching for his hand. She nuzzled it, tucking it under her cheek like a pillow.

He shifted his arm, trying to make it comfortable for her.

"Here," she said, "come up here with me."

She tried to make space for him, but the couch was narrow. He wound up more or less on top of her, his arms straining to support his weight.

"You can lie on me," she said, "I won't break."

He laid his head on her breast. She wrapped her arms around him.

He felt whole, or nearly whole.

"Are your parents still alive?" she asked.

"Maybe," he said. "But I don't think so."

"Do you miss them?"

"Yes," he said.

"I miss mine, too." She pulled his face to hers and kissed him. She shifted under him, freeing him with busy hands, then pulled her own clothes aside.

He felt for a time that he was drifting on a lake, the sunlight warm on his shoulders. He didn't want to hasten it, but his body moved anyway.

She strained against him, clasping with her thighs.

Afterward, they fell asleep.

She woke him a few hours later and led him to her bed. It was dark. His leggings had come unwrapped. He was embarrassed to be half naked in front of her.

She brought him a glass of water, which he drank in great gulps. She laughed and told him to save some for her.

They climbed under the sheets. He thought he might be dreaming, but her earthy smell was real enough.

Somehow she managed to guide him inside of her again. They moved together for a while, but it didn't build to anything. She kept stroking his face and asking about his childhood. He told her everything she wanted to know. He wasn't capable of holding back.

She listened, craning her neck to kiss him from time to time.

Then they were quiet together, but he couldn't sleep.

"Now it's your turn," he said.

She turned on the bedside light and held up her hand for his inspection. He traced an old scar in the meat of her palm. "Don't you recognize your own work?" she asked.

"Ah," he said, "you were my patient."

"I was just a girl," she said.

"Was I nice to you?"

"Very," she said.

"That's good. What else?"

"You knew my father." She said a name he didn't recognize. "That was his given name," she said, "but you knew him as the Magheed."

It was a name from a different life. It pierced him. "That's impossible," he said. "You can't be *that* Thali."

"Can't I?"

"I saw your business card."

"I took my mother's maiden name when I came to this country."

He shook his head. "Your father was the Magheed?"

"Yes," she said.

"You're *that* Thali?"

"Yes."

He was silent for a while. Her hand found his under the sheet.

"I should have been with him at the end," he said. "I could have protected him. At least I could have tried. But by the time I got back to the village, it was too late."

"They did him like a thief," she said, "but he wasn't."

"No, he wasn't."

He pulled his hand away. "I was a fool back then. I did things your father would have called *unclean*."

"I heard," she said.

"You did?"

"Yes."

Something grew in him until finally he blurted it out. "Did we just insult his memory?"

"Oh, Gus," she said. "My father admired you. He thought of you as one of us."

"I wanted to be. I tried."

"Well, you were and you weren't," she said. "Just like me."

He wanted to ask what she meant, but she yawned and said it was way past her bedtime. "Besides," she murmured, "it's almost time for work."

The building was waking up. He'd stubbed his toe on a plastic three-wheeler the other night, and now he heard a child racing it up and down the hallway. He lay still, trying to sense the faint vibrations of the wheels, the way he used to pause sometimes at dusk outside the camp, listening for thunder.

II

(TWENTY-ONE YEARS EARLIER)

1

*M*aster, my canoe boy asks, breaking the silence that has reigned between us for nearly an hour, *tell me again, what is your tribe?*

I don't have an easy answer for him. I could say my tribe is the occupying army, or the hospital staff, or my aging parents, who say they understand what I'm doing in the marshes, but keep agitating, year after year, for me to come home.

What I want to say is, *My people have evolved beyond tribes.* But to a marshman, that would be absurd. It would be like saying, *My people have evolved beyond hunger.*

A man must eat. Just so, a man must have a tribe.

But it's an earnest question, and earnest questions ought to be answered. *First of all,* I say, *how many times have I asked you not to call me master?*

He turns and smiles good-naturedly, as if I have praised and not chided him.

You and I are not so different, I say. *We both come from small tribes surrounded by strong enemies.*

It's an oblique answer. I'm not even sure what I mean by it myself. Sometimes the sentences run off on their own when I use the language of the marshmen.

He finds meaning in it anyway. I can tell he approves by the way his eyes narrow. My answer seems guileful to him, and guile is something the marshman respects.

Then, for the umpteenth time, he proceeds to recite his lineage, which is his way of scolding me for my lack of roots. He's talkative today. For two weeks, we've been living in close quarters, and he has respected my wish for quiet. But now the hunt is over. It's time to return to the field hospital. I've ordered him to turn us around—no small feat in the weed-choked channels, which are barely wide enough, in most places, to accommodate the sharp prow of my canoe.

The prospect of sleeping once again in his own hut has loosened his tongue. He narrates highlights of our hunt as if I hadn't lived them myself. *Five pigs!* he exclaims. *Who will believe we killed five pigs?* He digs a heel into our game bag, which is bulging with the day's coot. *A good hunt*, he says. He's proud of my shooting skills. I'm proud of his, too.

In a moment of enthusiasm, I call him by his nickname, Chigger, which makes his shoulders ripple with pleasure. He prefers that I use his official title, *canoe boy*, within earshot of his friends, but out here, with no one else around, we are at ease.

The long afternoon is over. The weed-strewn water has lost its oppressive glare. The sky is thick with fowl. There's a kind of relief in simply enjoying their flight, appreciating the noisy formations without worrying about sight lines or losing downed birds in impenetrable grass. *We are safe from you*, their eager honking seems to say. To which I feel like answering, *And we from you!*

The water has receded since the beginning of the hunt. Chigger tries mightily to avoid leaping in the shallow brine to free us when we run aground. It's a point of pride with him.

But the water is so low, and the towering reeds so thick, that at times we're both forced out of the canoe.

Progress along the waterway, which in places is hardly more than a brackish tongue of mud, is hard-won. It becomes clear, as evening lowers its shroud over the swaying grasses, that we will not reach home before dark.

Chigger wants to push on. His determination gives me pause. Perhaps he has taken a lover. And why not? He's young and handsome, and there's prestige in his long association with me. I wouldn't mind sleeping in my own bed, either. The comforts of camp have softened me. But it's unsafe to move in the marshes at night. This is unrelated to the occupation. Night in the marshes has been dangerous for thousands of years.

Where should we sleep? I ask.

Chigger protests in his gentle way, but I insist. Finally, he suggests a reed island in a nearby lagoon. *There will be shelter*, he says, *whether or not the villagers have carried.*

The marshmen are nomadic, moving from island to island as their buffalo exhaust the local fodder. Their mobility has always amazed me. They're capable of loading their households onto improvised rafts and vanishing into the reeds within minutes, if need be.

He doesn't wait for my assent. He knows I trust him implicitly in these matters. If he says there will be shelter, it will be there.

The reeds shudder as we part them. A purple gloom presses down their tips. Mallards call out overhead, inspiring Chigger to song, too, something about a girl with a gauze dress, and the tattoo on her thigh that can be seen through it.

Or perhaps it's a song of bride-stealing. The dialect is unfamiliar to me. In the gurgling near-darkness, the meaning of a monotonous song like this has a tendency to bend itself to one's mood.

Suddenly he squats. His bright palm flashes behind his back. This is our signal. There may yet be enough light to take another pig. Killing them is not mere sport. These wild pigs cause great hardship for the marshmen, rooting up their crops, trampling their goods, and causing a surprising number of fatal wounds with their filthy tusks.

I take up my cape gun and disengage the safety, which causes a new tension in the boat. Chigger's back glistens with exertion.

It's a moment of great intimacy between us, although he'd surely never describe it that way. Hunting accidents are second only to the resolution of blood feuds as a cause of death among the young men of the marshes.

The channel widens. He maneuvers the canoe to one side, then beaches it on ground that remains invisible to my eye even after the keel has bitten deeply into sand.

I follow him, staying close in the last of the light.

Pig? I whisper.

He nods, then spreads his arms wide. A large one.

And then we're on it. No sooner do we make out the hulking head, like an entire bristling beast itself, than the breeze shifts. The pig turns on us, shattering the peace of the evening with its roaring.

It charges, but the attack is merely a feint. By the time there's a clear line of fire, the pig is crashing away through the high grass.

We've missed a kill, but it's no great tragedy. The hunt was already complete. The violent atmosphere quickly dissipates. A cool breeze fluffs the grasses, restoring the calm.

But something's out of place. Chigger senses it, too. He touches my elbow and points to a shape on the ground where the pig was feeding, something dark and long laid out on the wet stubble. I ready the gun. It could be another pig, a juvenile.

As we approach, the breeze carries a familiar stench. It's not another pig after all, but the corpse of a young marshman, perhaps a few years older than Chigger.

The pig has been at the face. The forehead is split, and the scalp torn away. The cheeks are mostly gone. One ear remains, and just a bit of dark flesh where the nose was. The eyes have been eaten by something smaller. A crab, perhaps.

He was a sturdy young man, a rice farmer, by the look of his legs, which are scabbed up to the calf, the mark of a parasite common to rice paddies. Remarkably, the pig has spared the genitals, which exhibit a clean circumcision, the work of a surgeon,

not an itinerant barber. I've done countless circumcisions over
the years, enough to put most of those butchers out of business.
This young man was almost surely one of mine.

His belly is bloated, which suggests drowning, but drown-
ings are exceedingly rare among the marshmen, who learn to
swim practically before they can walk. A drowning is often a sign
of a drunken binge, but he seems too young and too poor for
that.

Chigger has retreated to the canoe. He wants no truck with
corpses. It's left to me to roll him over.

The wound across the forehead continues all the way around
the head, a ring of deep incisions like bird tracks. I haven't seen
anything like it since my early days here, when the use of razor
wire during interrogations was fairly common, a barbaric prac-
tice that has been banned for years.

Everything else points to an unlucky young rice farmer who
startled a wild animal. Perhaps the pig knocked him unconscious
with the first charge. I've seen it before. It has nearly happened
to me.

I'd like to be more definitive, but autopsies fall outside the
brief of our field hospital. Besides, the marshmen would never
warrant such a thing. They're pragmatic about death. As long as
there's a proper burial, they grieve fiercely, pounding their breasts
and wailing until one of them says, *Enough*. Then, as quickly as
it began, the keening ends. The grieving is set aside, erased with
the swiftness of the grass that closes behind a passing canoe.

Of all the marshmen's ways, it's the one I envy most.

We're in luck. The island Chigger mentioned is not far,
and, as he predicted, the villagers haven't decamped. We're welcomed by a naked boy hanging like a monkey from a brace of
bent reeds. The boy asks us, in a lovely pure treble, whether we've
eaten. This is the age-old greeting of the marshmen, a token of

their deep hospitality, but in the child's mouth it takes on the aggressive tone of a challenge.

Chigger berates him, telling him to hurry up and gather the elders.

The whole village receives us at the landing, arranged, like everything in these parts, by status. The man we need to see stands impassively by the guesthouse, which in this place is a modest hut that ordinarily stables buffalo.

We must make a bewildering sight: a paunchy foreigner dressed as a marshman, and a canoe boy with borrowed dog tags slapping his naked chest. Chigger parts the crowd, warning of what will happen if our welcome is not sufficiently warm.

But our purpose tonight is serious. I motion for him to be quiet, a gesture not lost on the villagers, who cross their arms with satisfaction to see the boy put in his place.

We have found a body, I say. *I would like to speak with the headman.*

This is a perversion of the normal order of things, which calls for a coffee ceremony before anything serious can be broached, but I don't mind trading on my status as an outsider. The rice farmer's family needs to be notified. Judging from the level of putrefaction, he's been missing for a while.

My announcement causes a general rush to the canoe. I'm left alone with the headman, who leads me into the guesthouse, where a young girl is seated in a place of honor by the hearth. Her cheeks are red from scrubbing. A brass chain has been hurriedly woven into her hair. I recognize the coin that dangles on her high forehead. It's military scrip, a copper blank stamped with the number five.

My host averts his milky eyes while I drink coffee and partake of some gritty rice. Then he takes the coffeepot from the girl and pours me another cup himself. The business with the corpse can wait. He imagines we're entering a bridal negotiation.

This is a very useful girl, he says.

I'm not looking for a wife, I say. The girl can't be more than eight years old.

He shrugs. The shrug is universal among the marshmen, a gesture with infinite subtle inflections. Here, it means, *Often a man doesn't know what he's looking for.*

A virgin, he says. *See for yourself.*

Father, I say, *I'm troubled about the rice farmer. Surely his people miss him.*

He frowns. I'm being difficult. The matter of the dead farmer will not be advanced by a foreigner's impatience. His grimace exposes a mouth empty of teeth except for one monstrous yellow canine. *Her mother is very fertile. She has five brothers.* He holds up three fingers, all that remain on the right hand, and supplements them with two fingers from his left. His withered arms tremble from the effort of holding up his hands.

Instead of marveling at the size of the girl's family, I thank him for the meal.

But he's not done. With the sour expression of a man who has been forced to play a valuable card prematurely, he leans in and confides, *Naturally, you want to know about the dowry.*

There's a commotion outside the guesthouse. Chigger appears, beckoning me with exaggerated gestures, so the villagers outside will have a clear idea of his influence.

A relative has been found, he says. *A cousin. The cousin has requested you.*

Requested me for what?

A consultation, he says.

I want to ask what there could possibly be to discuss, but I suppose I already know.

I apologize to the headman, then follow Chigger to the landing, where they've laid out the body in the sand. The cousin squats by the corpse, smoking nervously, shifting his weight from foot to foot like an inexperienced merchant rehearsing the price of his goods.

Here he is! Chigger announces.

On cue, the cousin pulls back the green army blanket, revealing the young man's ruined face. A nearby charcoal fire mercifully suppresses the odor.

The cousin rocks back and forth, puffing away with a disturbing air of detachment. Unless I'm mistaken, he's waiting for a pronouncement that will help set the blood price—not that one is warranted. This was an ordinary death, not a military one. No payment is due; nevertheless, here is the corpse, and here am I.

This is a side of life in the marshes that I understand, but despair of. What's really needed is to clean the young man and make him as presentable as possible before wrapping him in a winding sheet. All of this would have been automatic if it weren't for my presence.

The general hush is broken by a splash in the darkness, followed by an indignant snort. A child has thrown a stone at one of the wading buffalo. The animal churns the shallows in outrage, its broad back slick with moonlight. The boy laughs. Several of the elders scold him. There's even a halfhearted chase, but the boy is too nimble, and the men are confused by a foreigner in their midst.

Suddenly I feel the exertions of the hunt. My body aches. My face burns from long days of exposure. Without asking permission, I pick up the corpse and stagger with the stinking burden to the doorway of the guesthouse. If need be, I will clean him myself. But before I can enter, my way is barred.

Chigger explains the situation. Apparently, a single drop of the boy's blood has the power to render the reed structure ritually impure, and, with the recent conscriptions for levee work, there's simply not enough manpower to rebuild a guesthouse.

The corpse is leaden and incredibly rank. It takes all of my concentration to keep from gagging. I can feel body fluids seeping through to my skin. The faces here are all hostile. Even Chigger shakes his head with disapproval.

In the end, there's nothing to do but return the boy to his cousin, who hasn't budged from his place by the fire. He tilts his chin, indicating where he wants the body.

Everyone seems relieved that I've reestablished myself as an outsider. And not just an outsider. Let's not mince words.

An occupier.

2

We arrive back at camp at dusk the next day—that is, a day late. We haven't been missed. What is a day, or even a week, here in the marshes, where time is reckoned in terms of length-of-tour, often years?

Field hospitals are temporary by definition, but a more or less permanent village has formed around the perimeter of the camp, the way the great briny lakes here will precipitate a ring of salt along their shores. The marshmen come to camp for the wages. We hire them to avoid the more unpleasant of our daily duties. It's an age-old symbiosis, neither good nor bad, merely the vanguard of contact between two civilizations unequal in power. There hasn't yet been intermarriage, but it can't be far behind.

No marriage, but plenty of night sport, ever since the first heady weeks of conquest. I've been administrator here long enough to see lanky native children with the piercing green eyes of empire.

By my colleagues' suggestive smiles, I know that my tent girl is waiting for me. The adolescent smirking is hardly necessary. Of course she's waiting. That's what I pay her to do.

The tent is stifling. Our military tents don't breathe like the woven reed structures in the marshes. I've tried again and again to commission a guesthouse, but the marshmen will not build me one. Only a headman may commission a guesthouse. I'm a potentate, to be sure, but also a foreigner. I've offered an obscene sum of money, but the only takers have been good-for-nothings, drunkards who haven't the faintest idea how to work with reeds.

A common hut would suffice, but the marshmen refuse me even that. It's not considered proper for a potentate to sleep in a common hut. So instead of a light and airy haven, I'm welcomed by the bottled heat of my tent, redolent of bug spray and kerosene. The girl has laid out a rug for me and sits by it, her shapely legs tucked obediently to the side, a sweating clay pitcher of water in hand.

It is for me to speak first. *The hunt was good*, I say.

She welcomes me and readies my plate. When I tell her I'm too hot to eat, she clucks her tongue. It's the reaction of a much older woman, something she has seen her mother do, perhaps. She watches me very closely to make sure she hasn't overstepped. She's exceedingly lovely, but I find her youth off-putting. At times, I feel I'm playing house with a child.

She wouldn't be here at all if I hadn't intervened with some soldiers who were molesting her by the main gate. That night, I took her under my protection. We've been trying to agree on proper compensation ever since. Officially, she's my servant, but everyone assumes we're lovers. Such arrangements are the norm here. I don't bother trying to quell the rumors. Truth be told, her beauty has enhanced my reputation in the surgery.

She has asked me to call her "Betty," a name plucked from some fashion magazine. I would prefer simply calling her my tent girl, but she insists on the foreign name. *Tent girl* seems more honest to me. I wouldn't presume to call her by her marsh name, although surely an outsider would think that was more sensitive. Come to think of it, I don't even know her marsh name. I could find out easily enough, but that would feel like a kind of invasion. Imagine, being squeamish about such a petty invasion, after forcing open an entire country!

Betty pours me a cup of water and sits silently while I drink.

She's bursting with news, but it isn't the custom here to speak of news before a traveler has watered and fed.

The water is flat and metallic—"military grade"—meaning it has been boiled in one of the old brick ovens by the mess. I prefer the water the marshmen drink, despite its deplorable sanitation. It has never made me ill, at least not seriously, and I've always enjoyed the idea of drinking from the ancient river.

Betty used to be perfectly happy drinking river water, but now she'll only drink military grade. She's proud of this new affectation. I suppose she makes trouble when she visits her home village, demanding that her water be boiled. And they probably boil it for her. Being my tent girl has raised her status to the heavens.

She serves the meal, brushing me with her ample breasts as often as possible. It doesn't matter that I've said I'm not hungry. That's the way it is with her people. A marshman is always hungry, no matter how he might try to deny it.

Her arms move slowly, as if she has a secret aversion to the food she's serving. It isn't her turn to eat, but that's of no concern; neither will she eat later. She's very proud of her figure, and equally critical of the tent girls who let themselves go once they've created a stable position in camp.

Betty's cooking is lazy. It doesn't take much effort to boil a pot of rice and break a roasted chicken on top of it. I happen to know that she pays another woman to roast her chickens, but I don't mention it. She's easily embarrassed. Ours is not an intimacy that allows for much teasing.

I eat as much as I can, then announce that I'm tired and would like to sleep. In this kind of heat, I'd much prefer sleeping in the rough under some mosquito netting. But it wouldn't do for the administrator to be mistaken for a marshman in the camp. As comfortable as we've grown with each other, certain distinctions must be maintained.

Not long after I've stretched out on my pallet, Betty begins her predictable assault. Perhaps outside, in the stirring breeze, far from my gloomy thoughts about the rice farmer, I might be vulnerable to a gentle caress. But not here, in this oven of a tent. I tell her I'm too tired, which is true. I tell her the food is heavy in my belly.

She's put out. Her inability to arouse me is a blow to her prestige. Not that she cares for personal reasons. I know I'm unappealing to her. I've overheard her saying as much to her friends. I'm fat. I'm not jolly. I'm stingy with her allowance. She uses obscure marsh idioms to express all these things. Even if I don't understand the precise reference, I get the gist.

She takes my labored, heat-seared breathing as a sign of encouragement and redoubles her efforts. Her stroking is mechanical, as if she's milking a buffalo. That's what I am to her: a beast in need of tiresome milking. I feel the intensity of her gaze upon my cheek. If I were to become dissatisfied with her, the entire economy she has built around my patronage would crumble. She views the easy camaraderie I share with my canoe boys as a mortal threat.

I roll onto my stomach, which causes her at last to leave me in peace. She withdraws to her straw tick with a series of petulant sighs. Soon I hear her steady breathing. Betty falls asleep quickly and completely, like a true child of the marshes. I envy her this deep forgetful slumber, which seems to cover her in an imperturbable layer of silt.

She offers herself again the next morning. She perches on the edge of my pallet, opens her sleeping shift, and clasps her hands behind her head. I told her once that I thought she looked quite fetching lying that way, and now she uses the pose as a way of pressing her case: *This is what you like*, her sleepy eyes insist.

But I'm prepared for this. I rise and wash, and, while I'm up, fetch a gift from my knapsack, an ancient ceramic seal shaped like a cylinder, about the size of her forefinger.

This is for you, I say. I explain that it's probably three thousand years old. I point out the high-prowed canoe that has been incised in the clay. It looks just like mine, which was built only a decade ago. My voice catches as I tell her this. The way the marshman's culture has resisted the ravages of time moves me deeply.

She studies my offering with barely concealed disappointment. *Is it valuable?* she asks. Now it's my turn to shrug. I tell her I thought of her when I saw it. *You're very kind,* she says.

She fills me in on the camp gossip. One of my surgeons has impregnated his girlfriend, a thickset creature with enormous breasts and thighs, like the crude fertility figurines they sell as souvenirs in the port city. This is happy news for him. His wife back home is infertile. Now he'll have a child.

I ask Betty her opinion of the news. Does she imagine the surgeon will invite his tent girl to return home with him? Would the surgeon's wife accept such an arrangement? Is removing a child to a distant country as simple as transplanting an exotic tree?

But Betty has already moved on to the next subject. *That rice farmer you found was the son of a camp laundress,* she says. *Perhaps you've seen her in one of the lean-tos by the river.*

The speed at which news travels in the marshes has always amazed me. Early on, our forces spent considerable time and effort trying to disrupt the "reed telegraph," a vast informal web of communications that the insurgency used to great tactical advantage. The war planners soon realized it was hopeless; one might just as well try to silence the songbirds and crickets.

As for Betty's laundress, I have noticed washerwomen by the river, but never individually. The constant wet slap of laundry against boulders is a sound I accepted years ago and no longer even hear.

This laundress is trouble, she says. *She was born under an unlucky star.*

An unlucky star? I say. *Now you're a soothsayer?*

Betty leans over and rubs my upper lip with her thumb. *She has a cleft,* she says, drawing a V with her nail.

And girls with clefts are considered unclean. I use a very ugly word for "unclean," one usually reserved for whores.

Exactly, she says.

Now she has lost her son, I say. *Is that what she deserved, this laundress, for being born with a simple defect?*

We're both surprised by my vehemence. *No one deserves that,* Betty says, but it's clear she's unmoved by the laundress's loss. *You know,* she says, *in olden times, a cleft woman had it a lot worse. The whole tribe would heap its sins on her, and then, when they couldn't stand the sight of her any longer, they'd declare a feast day and stone her to death.*

And what do you make of this ritual? I ask, as neutrally as I can. Sometimes I tire even myself with this teaching impulse.

It hasn't happened for a long time, she says, yawning. *At least, not around here. I thought they still did it out in the bush, in places like the laundress's village, but I guess not.*

Betty can't wait for me to leave so she can take her morning nap. She stretches voluptuously, taunting me with flashes of pale private skin. She's fully aware of her powers. She thinks I'm a fool for pretending not to notice them.

A new general has taken command down at the palace, a modern ziggurat overlooking the river thirty kilometers south of us. They say he's "old school," this general; in other words, a stickler for rules. Before Chigger and I left for the hunt, I ordered the camp to be readied for a surprise inspection.

And now, the first morning back, I inspect it myself, asserting whatever authority is left in me. Usually, I walk at the head of a parade of noisy children, some of them in rags, but mostly naked, aping my stride and begging for spent cartridges, which the marshmen reload or, if the casing is too thin, hammer into jewelry. But today, children are banished from the dirt avenues, which have been smoothed and wet down for the occasion. The surface feels like the hard sand at the edge of an ocean, into which a foot can sink, but just slightly.

My tour starts with the soldiers' ward. There are only a few patients today: a wrist lacerated by a piece of reinforcing bar; a twisted ankle; and our current celebrity, an actual gunshot wound to the shoulder, the first such wound our sleepy hospital has seen since the first days of the occupation.

The patient is a big, jovial fellow, a former traveling salesman. He's a victim not of the insurgency, which can no longer be said to exist, but of his own corpsman, who drank himself unconscious, and then, woken by some fumbling in the dark, mistook friend for foe.

Despite our endless entreaties, the orderlies have thrown open the windows and filled the ward with flies. They've brought in a local boy and promised him a bounty for each dead fly. The orderlies are very proud of their system of pest control. They say it's to help the boy earn a bit of spending money, but I happen to know that the mother is one of the new dancing girls, fresh from the interior. No doubt she has promised her favors to the man who can bring her son closer to opportunities in camp.

He's a nice-looking boy, honey-skinned, long in the limb, respectful of the peace that hangs heavily over the empty beds. He has woven a flyswatter from some rattan skins. To make it look store-bought, like the tool of a professional fly hunter, he has lined the edges with black electrical tape.

His bare feet patter pleasantly on the concrete floor. He holds the swatter at attention, resting it on his shoulder like a little rifleman. His mother must have coached him to make a good impression on the administrator.

When I ask his name, and he answers, "Paul," the orderlies explode with laughter. The foreign name sounds pretentious to them.

I tell him that Paul is a fine name and thank him for helping to keep the ward sanitary.

He gives me a salute, then shows me his catch: a few dead flies at the bottom of a huge plastic jar, a cast-off from the mess. Perhaps it's the only vessel he could find, but I'd rather think of its size as a reflection of his eagerness, of a boundless desire to please.

After the soldiers' ward, I look in on the makeshift clinic where we treat marshmen, a mess tent that was pressed into temporary service years ago, but which has become a more or less permanent fixture. Treating the civilian population is strictly forbidden, with one exception: injuries related to combat. Of course, the case could be made that virtually all of the health problems we see fall into that category. Open hostilities may have ended long ago, but poverty and disease—stepchildren of the war—are endemic, and no less deadly than bullets or shrapnel.

It's an argument I've rehearsed over the years, but the truth is that no one really cares what we do up here on the northern border. Months go by when it seems we're all but forgotten.

Today, the clinic is quiet. A few elderly patients being treated for cirrhosis doze under sweating IV bags. Even the orderlies, usually a spirited and mischievous lot, have given in to torpor. The overhead fan has once again seized up. Everything is still, except for Paul, who creeps like a lizard behind the empty cots, hunting for flies.

The living quarters are my next stop. The officers have taken my orders seriously. Their tents have all been properly squared and swept. But then, they've always hired local women to do this work.

The soldiers' barracks, on the other hand, are as squalid as ever. It's nearly noon, and half the garrison is still lying abed. One of them eyes me insolently from behind a girlie magazine.

These bored, overmuscled lads have never listened to me. I can't really blame them; nevertheless, I launch into a speech about the new general. Just as I'm asking for their cooperation, one of the men interrupts me to announce that the laundry has arrived.

And, indeed, a monstrous basket of folded clothes floats through the doorway. Once inside, the basket begins its descent. It's an amazing balancing act: the laundress lowers a knee to the ground, then uses the prodigious power of her neck and shoulder to tilt the basket, very slowly, to the precise angle that allows her to slide it to her trembling thigh.

None of the men moves forward to assist her. Nor do I, for that matter.

Her face is modestly covered, but her eyes are red from weeping, and she wears a mourner's sash. The soldiers crowd around her, taking their clean clothes from the basket and tossing coins at her feet. As she scrabbles for them, one of the men holds a finger to his lips, sneaks up behind her, and snatches her headscarf.

Her arms fly up to cover her face while the soldiers play keepaway with the headscarf. The laundress is torn between the coins, which lie gleaming on the floor, and her scarf, which flutters like a raven among the men.

"Gentlemen," I say. "Give it a rest."

But the game is in full swing. Soldiers who a few minutes before were listless on their cots are now fully awake and shouting. Each wants his moment with the scarf.

It's innocent enough. They know nothing of this woman's loss. All they know is that they're bored; that here is a woman; and that teasing her offers a diversion from my tedious lecture.

This is just a game to them, which is why the roar of my sidearm comes as such a shock.

I turn to the soldier with the wadded scarf, whose arm is frozen in midair. "Give it back to her," I say.

But the laundress is gone. The gunshot has terrified her. She has fled, leaving basket and coins behind.

The soldiers are stunned. One of them waves a disbelieving hand through the shaft of sunlight created by the new hole in the roof. "Holy shit," says another.

I choose a scapegoat at random: a skinny, sunburned infantryman with a nasty-looking mole on his shoulder. It's all I can do to keep from examining it. The sun here is much more intense than in the homeland; melanoma is a constant worry.

I tell him to gather up the coins and the empty basket. He looks to his friends, but they have become stone-faced. The discharge of a weapon is an event with real meaning in their world, as opposed to the speechifying they're used to from me.

As we walk to the washerwomen's lean-tos at the edge of camp, I endeavor to explain. "Sometimes," I say, "teasing will go too far."

"Yes, sir."

"In the marshes, uncovering a woman like that is a grave insult. Typically, her face will remain hidden outside the home. She feels naked without her scarf. Do you understand?"

"Absolutely, sir."

The huge laundry basket extends awkwardly from his hip. It's truly ungainly, except when balanced on the head of a marshwoman, where its design reaches a kind of perfection.

"I'm not sure you do," I say. "Are you prepared to marry this laundress?"

"No, sir, I am *not* prepared to do that!" Suddenly he's standing at attention.

"Then don't undress her," I say, dismissing him.

His retreat to the barracks is an out-and-out sprint. Talk of marriage has truly frightened him. His panic would be amusing if it weren't so sad. To a soldier of the garrison, marrying a woman from the marshes would be an abomination. While marshwomen certainly have all the requisite parts to be useful on a Saturday night, they aren't considered fully human. I've actually heard our soldiers refer to the marsh people as "mudmen," as if they'd been shaped from the red clay but denied the divine breath that would give them a soul.

It takes the better part of an hour to find the laundress. The heat is dizzying, and there's precious little shade in the flats. The lean-tos are full of nattering women who go silent when I come crashing by. Bursts of shrill laughter follow me down the path.

I come upon her suddenly in a shabby lean-to set apart from the others. I duck under the roof and there she is, radiating all the stubborn energy of a beast surprised in a field. She's wearing a new headscarf improvised from a rag. It's bright red, a foreign color, but it suits her. Her fine dark eyes seem to glow in the narrow slit.

I brought your scarf, I say, *and your basket. This is yours, too, I believe.* I place a stack of coins on the edge of the folding table, hoping she won't notice that I've added a few to the pile myself.

She counts the coins, taking only what she was owed, and hands back the rest. Then she returns to her folding, a great pile of soldiers' fatigues.

I watch her for a while. The rhythm is mesmerizing. Her hands are very precise. I tell her I admire her skill.

She contradicts me with the slightest shake of her head.

The pile of fatigues grows and grows until it looks ready to topple. I step in, but the only result of my intervention is to drive her nervously into the corner.

I'm sorry, I say, *I'll leave you be.*

Then, with a movement so abrupt that for a moment I think she has tripped, she prostrates herself at my feet.

What's this? I ask, bending to help her up. My senses sharpen. Someone might walk in and see us this way. *Come, now*, I say, but she insists on pressing herself to the ground.

Please, Master, she says. She stops for a moment, overcome by emotion. *I would like to have my son back.*

I've heard about your loss, I say. *I saw to the boy myself.*

She thanks me, but it's the kind of thanks one might give a merchant who offers a paltry refund for some spoiled meat. I wait for more gratitude, but something else comes: a question, tinged with rage. *Are you finished with him, then?*

Please get up, I say. *You're embarrassing me.*

I help her to her feet. She sighs. Her knees crack as she straightens. She isn't old, but brute labor has already worn out her joints. She looks at me with defeated eyes.

Perhaps I've misunderstood, I say.

I would like to bury my son, she says.

If it's a question of money . . .

She answers with supreme disdain. *His body was taken away*, she says. *They came in the night.*

Who came?

Soldiers, she says.

What soldiers?

She touches the stack of fatigues. *From this tribe*, she says.

I try to take her hand, but she pulls back. *I will look into it*, I say.

She doesn't believe me. She thinks I've merely employed one of the empty phrases my people use to dismiss a claim, a phrase as formulaic as the ones the other laundresses probably used to acknowledge her grief.

You will have your son back, I say. *You have my word.*

She bows awkwardly, then steps outside and waits for me to leave.

I'm as astonished by my impulsive promise as she is. I haven't given my word in a very long time. I wouldn't have thought I was still capable of it.

3

The palace has changed since my last visit. The new general has remilitarized it. My relic of a jeep, with its sandblasted hood and steaming radiator, is stopped at no fewer than three checkpoints. A fresh road has been laid in a defensive spiral that forces all traffic to circle the compound twice before coming to a halt at the main gate. The uncured asphalt causes trouble for the jeep's nearly bald tires, which squeal as they negotiate the road's constant inward curve.

Inside the gate, the frame of a new building, a flat sprawling hulk with partitions for countless tiny rooms, rises from a sea of razor wire. The parade ground is jammed with camouflaged construction equipment. Jogging soldiers reach out and slap the giant tires to the rhythm of ribald exercise songs.

The great columns and arcades of the palace are festooned with patriotic banners. The messages are fragmentary and oblique. THIS IS YOUR MISSION! says one. UNTIL WE'RE VICTORIOUS! says another. The fabric is something I've never seen before, a gossamer mesh that iridesces like a locust's wing. I'm forced to avert my eyes when the desert wind lifts it to the sun.

The general is out riding, which gives me a chance to cool off in the cavernous waiting area outside his office. It's rumored that virtually every room of the palace, which was built atop the ruins of an ancient ziggurat, was used, at one time or another, by the torturers of the old regime. One imagines cries of agony echoing down the polished corridors.

When I'm summoned, at long last, into the general's office, I find a familiar face.

"Administrator," he says, pressing my arm.

"Is that Curtis?"

"*General* Curtis," he says, tapping the star on his collar. The uniform is new to me; black and severe, the sleeves embroidered with the blazon of Protective Services. "Sorry to keep you waiting. Have a seat. Tell me, has it really been ten years?"

He retreats behind the immaculate sandstone desk. His wavy blond hair is neatly trimmed—although longer than it should be, for a stickler for the rules—and the beard is gone, but he's just as vital as I remember. If anything, with his cheeks flushed from the exertions of the ride, and his face a bit fuller, he looks even younger than before. I, on the other hand, feel like a tired old man. "Forgive the impromptu visit," I say.

Curtis smiles and repeats the word "impromptu," shaking his head. "One forgets there are educated men out here," he says.

As I explain my purpose, he tries to give the impression that his attention is fully focused, but he can't resist polishing his high leather boots with a thumb, which he surreptitiously wets from time to time.

"An unhappy story," he says, "although I'm not sure I buy it. It's highly unlikely a random corpse would have found its way to our morgue. But you're welcome to have a look." He reaches for the intercom, then thinks the better of it. "Actually, I'll take you down myself," he says. "There's something I want you to see."

A lurching service elevator delivers us to the bowels of the palace, where Curtis leads me through a warren of utility tunnels. It's a struggle to keep up with his energetic strides. In the hope of slowing him down a little, I offer my congratulations.

"What for?" he says.

"Your promotion. This posting."

Curtis tilts his head, listening for irony in my voice. "Frankly," he says, "I was surprised to hear you're still camping on the border after all these years. A man of your talents, with those incredible language skills."

"I like running a field hospital. It makes me feel useful."

"Really, Gus," he says, as if we're old friends, "it's a waste of you."

Then he stops in front of a pair of steel doors. "Well, here we are."

"The morgue?" I ask, but he merely smiles and opens a door for me.

I hesitate at the threshold. The air is wet and musty. It's pitch-black inside, but there's a sense of vast space, as if the doorway gives out on a canyon.

"The lights are just . . . here," he says, throwing a lever. Arc lamps, some of them at a great distance, slowly start to blaze, illuminating a massive stone ruin at our feet.

"My predecessor was excavating for a weapons bunker when the ground under one of the earthmovers gave way. That was how they found the first chamber. Took the better part of six months to clean the whole thing out."

"What is it?"

"Guess," he says.

The intricate foundation reminds me of a picture from one of my old schoolbooks. "Steam tunnels, perhaps for the royal baths?"

"Good guess! A very good guess. But no. It's a labyrinth."

"A labyrinth? Here? Can we take a closer look?"

Curtis nods indulgently and says, "I knew you'd like it."

As we climb down and pick our way, single file, along a tightly curving path, he explains that most people have the wrong idea about labyrinths.

"The classical ones weren't really mazes," he says. "They were more like spirals: one way in; one way out."

He goes on to say that the labyrinth inspired the design of the new defensive road around the compound. "You see? I'm still capable of learning a thing or two from this godforsaken place."

There's a surprising amount of regret in his voice. This may be as close as I'll ever get to an apology.

Long years among the marshmen have taught me to hold my tongue. In the old days, I might have lashed out at him: *Save it for the child who lay screaming on my table!* But there's no point in saying such a thing to Curtis, a man so lacking in humility. Then again, perhaps I lack it, too, for presuming to stay in the marshes, for presuming to atone.

I walk on in silence, trying not to turn an ankle on the uplifted cobbles.

When we reach the center of the labyrinth, a clearing barely large enough to exercise a horse on a tight tether, Curtis tries again. "Things are different now," he says. "We have new methods. It's much easier. I can always use a good man, a trusted man. There's everything here: books, music, wine. I even brought a chef with me, a miracle-worker with wild game. Surely you miss the creature comforts."

"I do, but I'd miss the hunting more."

"You could still hunt!" he says. "You could certainly hunt. So, if hunting were part of the mix—"

He breaks off when he sees the expression on my face. "Fine," he says, raising his hands in surrender, "do what you want. Maybe someday you'll explain it to me."

In fact, we understand each other perfectly. He wants to keep me close, if only to ease his conscience; whereas I want no part of his methods, old or new. The very phrase "new methods" makes my gorge rise.

"Well," he says, "there's no need to go back the way we came."

He leads me through a series of concealed doors that provide a more or less direct path through the stone spiral. Soon we're back out in a modern hallway, where the way to the morgue is clearly marked.

Curtis isn't used to taking no for an answer. He sees my refusal as yet another misstep in a second-rate career. "Well," he says, slapping dust from his trousers, "*someone* has to clean up this mess."

"What mess would that be?"

He deflects the question with a roll of his eyes, as if to say, *You have no idea.*

To change the subject, I ask about the new building going up inside the gates.

"Finally, a proper detention facility," he says. "Long overdue. Now watch yourself," he adds, plowing through a heavy swinging door.

The sudden drop in temperature is like a plunge into water. Curtis cranes his neck. "There's usually an attendant," he says. "But it looks like we're on our own."

He slows to a funereal pace when we reach the storage area. It's clear that he means the tragic rhythm of the drawers to arouse my patriotism, but instead I find myself thinking about the marshman's horror of being unburied, which is considered the violation of violations. To abandon the body of a warrior on the battlefield—even a warrior of a rival tribe—is to cover one's own tribe in shame.

"In case you're wondering," he says, "these drawers are full."

"How is that possible?" I ask. "We haven't seen combat casualties in a very long time."

"You're privy to a tiny corner of this conflict," he says. "And even that you don't see with the proper vision." He stops to open one of the drawers. The corpse is charred, its lips curled in a dry snarl. "As a matter of fact," he says, "there's been a steady uptick in insurgent attacks."

He opens more drawers. The bodies are riddled with shrapnel, the wounds packed with sandy debris. Some of the remains are tragically scant—a blasted jawbone, a bloodied sleeve. Many lack dog tags.

"Are we sure these are ours?" I ask.

Curtis tries to slam the drawer, but it wasn't designed to be closed in anger. It recoils against rubber bumpers, then quietly slides home. "There's a separate section for the enemy down at the end," he says. "Knock yourself out."

In fact, the INSURGENT area is full to overflowing. I find two or three corpses crammed into each drawer, sometimes haphazardly, sometimes head to toe, their broken limbs woven together to save space. At first, I do my best to separate them, straighten their clothes, cover their desiccated eyes, but even these slight changes cause the drawers to jam. As I force them shut, the sound of cracking bone makes me think of the laundress.

After an hour of fruitless searching, followed by another lost to the seemingly identical tunnels under the palace, I finally reach daylight. I've never been so happy to climb into my oven of a jeep. The spiral road winds me up and flings me into the desert. I don't breathe freely until the jagged silhouette of the palace vanishes from the rearview mirror. Dust devils race me down the pitted road.

This used to be a perilous drive, seeded with mines and improvised explosives. The surface has been patched but still gives a vehicle a good beating. As I near home, my wheels seem to gather speed. It's like I'm driving down a ramp through the centuries.

That night, I wonder: Is there really a new insurgency? The question sits, indigestible, in the pit of my stomach, as Betty snores quietly in her corner. I may be a foreigner, but with every wound I've sewn, every child I've bathed, I've tried to come closer. I lie on a sweat-stained quilt, thinking, *I'm bound to them, but are they bound to me?*

Eventually, sleep comes, but it's disturbed by a vision of the laundress kneeling by my bed, holding a candle to her naked mouth. The guttering flame lights her face like a jack-o'-lantern, grotesquely hooking her nose, deepening her eye sockets, but above all, transforming the cleft in her lip into something huge and malignant. *I've been thinking about a surgery*, she says.

Her words fill me with joy. I want her to be joyful, too, but her eyes are black and bottomless, as inscrutable as river stones.

I wake to find Betty hovering over me. *You've been blubbering*, she says. *You shouldn't drink so much before bed. But don't worry*, she whispers, wiping my face with the sleeve of her shift, *your secret's safe with me.*

A letter from Protective Services arrives by courier the next day, informing me that a claim of corpse-stealing is an ancient form of extortion in the marshes; that there have been many substantiated cases of insurgents perpetrating abominations while dressed as our soldiers; and that, in any case, the laundress's son was a known insurgent with several atrocities to his name.

I'm to cease my inquiries into this matter, to focus on the efficient management of the field hospital, and, in a final phrase that makes me wince, to "desist in the delivery of medical services to the insurgency and its shadow army of supporters, *no matter the cause of injury.*"

In other words, I'm to stop treating marshmen.

"Shadow army," "atrocities," "abominations"—the language alone is infuriating. Do the deskbound mandarins who compose these letters even know what the words mean? "Desist in the delivery of medical services," indeed! If a child is brought to me whose leg has been blown off by an old land mine, I'm to refuse treatment? Is that refusal not an atrocity?

I spend the day at my desk composing indignant replies,

each more self-righteous than the last, but reason ultimately prevails. I'm already on thin ice with Curtis, and the thought of being transferred fills me with dread. Perhaps it's selfish to wonder what will become of my marshmen when I'm gone, but I worry all the same.

Evening finds me standing in front of a mirrored armoire, the brass buttons of my old dress whites winking back at me, a worn leather belt straining to cinch my gut.

I'm all too aware of the ridiculous figure I cut on the long walk to the lean-tos. Dark patches of sweat blossom under the arms of my ill-fitting jacket. It's not healthy for a man to feel such shortness of breath, such palpitations.

I find the laundress fully absorbed in her work folding tattered tunics and leggings. Native laundry. The other laundresses have apparently stepped in and taken the soldiers' custom. It's cruel, but this is the way of the marshes. A woman, marked for punishment at birth, has simply been served another portion of her curse.

Waiting for news has been very hard on her. In a voice barely above a whisper, she offers me a cup of river water, then turns back to her folding.

I tell her about my trip to the palace, making more of my search than there actually was. Then I show her the letter forbidding me to look any further into her son's case. I read from it, translating as I go. I stop at the part about his being an insurgent, but in the end, I blurt it out anyway, then immediately distance myself from the allegation.

She waits for more. Her hands stay busy with threadbare work clothes, folding them automatically, but eventually slowing, like a hall clock winding down.

Ghilad was a good boy, she says.

I'm sure he was, I say. It's strange to hear his name in the solemn quiet of the lean-to, without the reassuring clatter of a typewriter or the rustle of an official form.

The other farmers teased him because of me, she says, *but they all envied his crops.*

Was he an only child? It's an awkward question at this late stage, an oversight on my part that reflects a larger truth: the everyday life of this woman has no real significance in the occupiers' bureaucracy.

I had a daughter, too, she says. *A talented seamstress. She was killed in the first days of the invasion, but they never told me how.*

Two children lost to the war; both unburied.

I take her in my arms. She doesn't fight me; neither does she melt into my embrace. She goes limp, a defenseless animal in the clutches of a predator.

I whisper an apology, but it comes out in my language, not hers.

My face is suddenly hot and wet. I feel her trembling. It isn't grief, or anger, or even—heaven help me!—desire, that makes her tremble. It's my tears. I doubt she's ever seen a man cry, and surely not a foreigner. She's afraid. Or perhaps merely embarrassed.

I kneel before her, clutching her knees like a schoolboy, pressing my face into her damp skirt, and say, *I made you a promise. I mean to keep it.*

Her hands eventually come to rest on my head, but don't know what to do there. They flutter for a while, then are still.

The laundress waits outside my tent, squatting like a woman who wishes to be swallowed by the earth. Betty will have nothing to do with her.

That creature doesn't belong here, she says.

Nevertheless, I say, *I have brought her.*

The camp won't stand for it.

We both know she's simply expressing a personal revulsion. *I want you to prepare a pallet for her*, I say.

Betty's hands fly to her face as if I've slapped her. *So now I'm to be her servant?*

No, she's our guest. I'm asking only that you be hospitable.

You're the one who's inhospitable, she says, gathering her things. Then, with all of her worldly goods bundled in her arms—along with a few of my own, I notice—she turns to me and says, *I hope she pleases you.*

On her way out, she spits on the laundress, who accepts the insult with a meek bow.

I'm very sorry about that, I say, dabbing her with a handkerchief before leading her into the tent and sitting her down on the edge of my bed. *I want you to be comfortable here. If there's anything you need, just tell me. I'm counting on you to do that.*

She nods, still in a fog. By bringing her to my tent, I've elevated her to a dizzying height.

I give her water and a bar of chocolate. She sips mechanically, but doesn't unwrap the chocolate, so I do it for her. *It's good,* I say, *very sweet.* She refuses. She cannot eat before I do.

I take a bite of the chocolate, which is soft and messy. I try to make it seem delicious, but honestly, the sweetness is too much in the heat.

Now you, I say, holding out the bar. Eating is very private for her; she manages the scarf with great skill.

The taste makes her wince. She gives the bar back, then turns away and takes a long drink of water.

No? I say. *That's all right. We'll find something you like. Why don't you lie down now? You should rest.*

She begins to undress in front of me. She's already half naked by the time I realize what's happening.

I stay her arms, then cover her with my jacket. What I want to do is to stroke her hair and keep watch over her. But touching her, no matter how chastely, would only add to her confusion. So instead, I ask about Ghilad. *If we're to make a case,* I say, *I must know all the facts.*

She shakes her head. She doesn't want to talk about her son. She's not interested in making a case.

Do you know what a case is? I ask.

In her mind, the matter is simple. We must find the potentate who has power over her son's corpse. We must borrow money to pay him. Then we must figure out how to pay back the enormous debt.

That's how it works here, I say, *but not in my homeland. For us, justice isn't a matter of bribes.*

She tells me she doesn't want justice. She only wants a proper burial for her son.

All of the talking has upset her. I give her a mild sedative and wait until she's asleep. Then I summon Chigger. Quietly, so as not to disturb my new guest, I tell him to go to the laundress's village and find out everything he can about Ghilad.

4

By the time Chigger returns, the laundress and I are the talk of the camp. As Betty predicted, I've become something of an outcast. My patients no longer encourage me to linger in the ward. Even the junior officers avoid me. They can understand, and even envy, a beautiful tent girl; a laundress, on the other hand—and a cleft one, at that—smacks of desperation.

The marshmen have begun to avoid me as well, except for Paul, the little fly catcher, who faithfully shows me his jar, all the while hinting that he's ready for a promotion: he wants to be my new bodyguard. I ask him if he thinks he's brave enough. He tells me he isn't afraid of anyone. He shows me a knife he made from the leaf spring of an old jeep, a miniature version of the marshman's ubiquitous curved dirk. He slashes the air with it, cursing my enemies.

There's a rumor in camp that I've cut Betty off, but it's not true. I've kept up her allowance. She hasn't suffered since she left my tent. She's gone on to become a popular entertainer at the canteen, where she sings songs full of thinly veiled references to me, hinting that I'm impotent, a pedophile, that she used to force me to wear a skirt while I slavishly painted her toenails. The songs are lively and witty, and Betty sings them well. Part of me is glad to see her make something of herself, even if it comes at my expense.

Chigger finds me in the hospital yard, sitting on a bench in the barren patch where the marshmen's tent used to stand. I've taken to spending my evenings there, often with a drink in hand and a bottle by my feet.

In the two weeks he's been gone, Chigger seems to have grown a full inch. He approaches slowly, studying the sandy ground. I make space for him on the bench. *Sit*, I say, but today he prefers to stand at attention with his hands clasped behind his back. I notice that he hasn't bothered to shave.

Have you eaten? I ask.

I'm not hungry, he says.

Not hungry? Since when are you not hungry?

Then he salutes like one of the soldiers from the barracks. Very odd.

Come, Chigger, I say, *we'll have a drink together and you can tell me about your trip.*

My invitation poses a dilemma. I can see that he wants to blurt out his report and go, but he's seduced by the idea of a cool drink.

Marshmen aren't welcome in the officers' club, so I take him to the canteen. Even there, he and I aren't wanted. By the time I've ordered our drinks and returned to the table, several of the soldiers have left. The radio has been switched off, along with the ineffective electric fan, whose red streamers flutter and go limp.

I hand Chigger one of the soft drinks he loves so much. He sets it on the table and picks at the label.

I thought you liked this brand, I say. I'm trying not to lose my patience, but really, this new behavior is childish in the extreme. Where, I wonder, has the old Chigger gone?

I like beer now, he says nonchalantly, casting a sidelong glance at me to see how I'll react.

Beer is not good for you, I say.

You mean they don't serve my kind alcohol, he says.

No. I mean that beer is not good for you. Since when do you tell me what I mean? Or imply that I haven't spoken my true mind?

Chigger blushes, but holds his head defiantly. He really has undergone an amazing transformation.

So tell me, I say, trying to assume the old tone of familiarity, *what did you learn?*

He opens the soft drink thoughtfully, using his strong white teeth as a bottle opener. It makes me cringe to see him do it, but I hold my tongue.

I learned plenty, he says slyly, *but it was expensive.*

Stop it, I say.

Stop what? he asks.

Stop acting like—

A marshman?

Like a scoundrel.

He frowns, then raises his bottle and gulps it down.

Tell me about Ghilad, I say. *They claim he was an insurgent.*

Perhaps he was.

Meaning?

Chigger holds up the empty bottle. *I'm still thirsty*, he says.

Chigger starts by explaining that the rice farmer relies on water for the propagation of his crop. I don't interrupt him, although I know far more about rice farming than he does. I want him to keep talking. Talking seems to be a cure. He's more like himself with every word.

The trouble began, Chigger says, at the beginning of the rainy season, when the seedlings had just been transplanted and needed to be kept wet. Ghilad paid his headman, as always, for his allotment of water, but when it was time for his field to be flooded, he learned that the headman had accepted his payment in bad faith. A new levee was under construction. There was no more water to be had; not in that season, or any season in the future.

I'm not familiar with this new levee, I say. *Is it military or civilian?*

Chigger shrugs, holding out his palms like a set of scales. *That's neither here nor there*, he says. Ghilad simply did what any marshman would do. One night, he took a pick and shovel to it, and by morning, his fields were properly flooded. As they always had been in the past, year upon year.

Remember, Chigger says, as if the whole story turns on this crucial point, *he'd paid his headman for the water!*

The headman complained to the army's regional commander, who dispatched a crew to patch the levee and reinforce it with concrete.

Ah, I say, *a military levee.*

Chigger pauses for dramatic effect. His eyes take on a priestly seriousness. *How*, he asks, *will Ghilad overcome this new obstacle?*

The answer lies in cheap concrete: too much sand, too much gravel, nowhere near enough cement—scarcely stronger than dried mud! The occupying army has been tricked again, this time into buying substandard concrete. It's a reliable comic turn for a story among the marshmen.

A few blows with a sledgehammer, followed by another night's work with pick and shovel, and the water is flowing again.

But this second breach is taken more seriously. An attack on an earthen levee is one thing. An attack on a levee reinforced not just with concrete, but with the faith and credit of the army of occupation, requires a response.

Why don't I know about this levee?

Chigger frowns at my interruption, then continues his tale. The regional commander answers with a third levee of high-quality reinforced concrete, with a tower overlooking Ghilad's fields, and hires watchmen from a rival tribe.

Unfortunately, he says, *Ghilad can't count on support from his tribe, thanks to his mother's cleft lip. And without it, a lone marshman is powerless against these kinds of forces.*

By this, I understand Chigger to mean the forces of fate, not the levee and watchtower, which are merely its agents.

Nevertheless, Chigger says, *he does not bow down.*

Ghilad's final act of insurgency involves explosives. The cost of this black market ordnance, filched from an army depot, is staggering. To pay for it, he borrows a fortune at usurious rates. Not only that, but the reinforced concrete is difficult to penetrate with sledgehammer and pick. When morning comes, Ghilad is forced to abandon his digging and plant the explosives in a shallow hole.

The sentries find the homemade device and attempt to defuse it, but they're clumsy. There's an explosion. No one is killed, but one of them loses a thumb and three fingers to the blast. As luck would have it, the maimed man turns out to be a part-time informant for the occupiers, with nearly the status of an occupying soldier himself.

What was there to do? Chigger asks. *Ghilad ran and hid. Despite his unpopularity, some saw him as a freedom fighter, although with a poor understanding of the larger conflict. In the end, someone must have turned him in. A marshman who doesn't wish to be found is like a reed among reeds.*

I've never heard Chigger use the phrase "freedom fighter." It's chilling. Even worse is the admiration in his voice.

What if the maimed man were from your tribe? I ask. *Would you feel differently?* Chigger answers carefully, as if the soldier sweeping the floor behind us were secretly a court stenographer. *There is merit on both sides*, he says. *But the stars favor the farmer, whose work is more honest.*

It's a shrewd answer, delivered in the manner of a soothsayer. Chigger has a great future as a headman, if there's any power left in his people's hands when his time comes.

One of the native porters, a wiry man I once treated for a burst eardrum, comes to fetch me the next morning. I invite him into the tent, but he refuses, looking nervously over my shoulder for any sign of the laundress.

The general is here, he says, dashing off like a frightened child.

The whole camp has turned out for the inspection, which is under way in the hospital yard. Curtis has brought one of his mounts, an immense stallion imported from the homeland, the better to impress the soldiers of the garrison, who vie with one another to have a picture taken by his saddle.

He cuts a fine figure on his steed. Even the marshmen are impressed, although they watch the proceedings from a safe distance. All except Paul, who clamors for the general's attention as eagerly as any of the soldiers. And in fact they pass him forward on their shoulders. He has become a kind of mascot.

Curtis acknowledges the boy with a crisp salute. The men applaud the gesture. This exchange between their general and the obedient marsh boy can only be a good omen.

One of the soldiers takes the general's reins and points in my direction. Curtis thanks him, then trots over, waving farewell to the men with his pristine cap. Their faces glisten with the heat of the day. It has been a long time since they wore their uniforms buttoned up, with proper shoes on their feet.

Curtis is glowing, too, as he climbs down to greet me. It's easy to see why he inspires such loyalty. He loves fighting men, even lazy ones like ours.

"Administrator," he says offhandedly, rubbing the horse's jaw. "Does the camp meet with your approval?"

"Actually, I'm here to have a word about that rice farmer."

We walk to the communal trough, where Curtis pumps water for his horse, stroking its flanks contemplatively as it drinks. Most mornings there's a long line at the water, but today it's deserted. Marshmen are surely watching, though.

"There's been a misunderstanding," I say. "He wasn't insurgent."

"No?" Curtis asks, picking a burr from the horse's twitching ear. "What would you call him, then?"

"A farmer trying to water his crops. The source of the problem seems to have been a water dispute."

"No," Curtis says, "the source of the problem was a lack of respect."

"Watering a field is hardly an act of war."

"That's debatable," he says, squinting at the sun. "At any rate, there was indeed a misunderstanding. We're not in the business of returning insurgent remains. Sends the wrong message. My men shouldn't have abandoned the corpse. As soon as they were informed of their error, they rectified it."

He reaches into a saddlebag and pulls out an envelope with a paltry amount of scrip. "This is for the mother," he says. "It's more than she's entitled to. Make it clear that this is the end of it. And another thing," he says, climbing back into the saddle. "You're going to be working with us again, just like before. It's either that, or you're finished here."

Steadying myself with the reins, I ask, "What if she wants to know where her son is buried?"

Curtis takes them from my hand and says, "Tell her to follow the crows."

I spend the day raising cash—emptying my strongbox, calling in old loans, even selling my precious cape gun to a surgeon who has long coveted it. At dusk, I'm at the lean-tos, my pockets bulging with bills. The laundress is perched on a boulder by the river, bathing her feet in muddy water. A heap of soiled laundry lies untouched nearby in a basket.

I spoke with the general, I say, showing her the sheaf of bills. *He wants you to have this.*

She looks wistfully at the money, but doesn't take it.

I sit down next to her, but there isn't room. I slip, sinking to the ankle in warm muck.

Is there anyone more powerful? she asks.

No, I say.

Then Ghilad is lost?

Take this, I say, forcing the money into her hand. *We can still have a burial. We'll bury his favorite things. I've heard of people doing it that way.*

No, she says firmly. Aggressively, even. *That kind of thing isn't for us.*

5

Toward morning, there's a distant rumble. I bury my face in my pillow, dreaming of the sudden downpours that scour the grasses at the edge of the lake, releasing their musk.

But the rains haven't come. A few moments later, the gelid ground heaves.

Officers and porters pour out of their tents half dressed. The word "earthquake" is in the air, but then someone spots a column of fire on the horizon in the direction of the gas pipeline.

This isn't the first time the pipeline has been breached. The thieves lack the tools to cut it safely. They use hammer drills, grinders, sometimes even torches. A crowd will have gathered in anticipation of free fuel. There will be casualties.

Soon the first makeshift ambulance arrives: a flatbed truck. We smell the wounded before we see them. Third-degree burn victims, seven of them, their clothes still smoking. Of these, three are dead, three are critical, and one is a hysterical toddler fused to his mother's thigh by a melted jerrican. The mother is dead, the flesh on her back burnt down to the spine. It seems she died protecting the child from the blast. It's horrifying and heart-rending and we cut them apart and move on.

The next group arrives in the back of a poultry truck, piled in among reeking crates. Then another truck arrives, and another. The ward overflows into the yard, which is soon heaped with empty burn kits.

As the hours pass, the cries intensify, assaulting the ears like a flock of starlings that never settles. At a certain point, I look up to find an armored convoy barreling down on us. Personnel carriers skid to a halt in front of the hospital, raising clouds of dust. We cover our patients as best we can while soldiers from Protective Services dismount and race across the grounds. Their trucks are left idling. Diesel fumes fill the air, even as the dust settles.

I approach the drivers and ask them to shut off their engines, but they refuse to hear me. They don't even roll down their windows.

The soldiers move in sudden evasive spurts, taking cover where they find it, as if this were a battlefield.

Fine, I think, *let them play at their war-making*. I have a hospital to run.

Then one of my surgeons comes to tell me that patients are being removed from the ward.

"And taken where?" I ask.

The surgeon shrugs. His hands are covered in gore and burn ointment. I hold a canteen to his lips. He drinks it dry, then tells me that we're dangerously low on everything.

I spot a pair of guards bearing a wounded marshman and rush over to them.

"Here!" I say. "Where are you taking this man?" But they ignore me, too. I might as well be a ghost.

I follow them to a metal shipping container mounted on a flatbed. The doors of the container shift like vanes in the breeze. The air is alive with cries of agony, but of a different sort from the ones I've heard all morning.

The soldiers heave the patient into the container, then race back to the hospital with their empty stretcher.

I peer inside, where a dozen marshmen are laid out in a row, their hands bound with bright plastic restraints. In the depths of the container, an officer is setting up an arc lamp. I recognize him by the pale eyes and delicate mustache as a man named Reiff, one of Curtis's adjutants. When we first met, he was a gunnery sergeant; now he wears the uniform of a lieutenant colonel.

Reiff aims the lamp at a bearded elder whose torso has been ravaged by the explosion. The man's blackened rib bones are thrown into stark relief; the raw fibers of his intercostal muscle glint as he breathes. There's a lot of shouting, but Reiff's language skills are poor. I can barely make out the words, and only because I know how to adjust for his foreign accent.

Then he reaches in his pocket and produces a miniature plumber's torch, which he lights with a flourish. He adjusts the flame to a brilliant blue pinpoint, then kneels and holds it to the elder's open wound.

The marshman lets out a bloodcurdling cry. The others cry out, too, like dogs howling in response.

"Reiff!" I shout.

Reiff turns to me, his face purple with heat and exertion. "It's Gus, right?" he asks. "The king of jibber-jabber? You'd better get in here."

"These men belong in the ward."

Reiff smiles sardonically. "Curtis warned me about your bullshit," he says.

"They need to be moved. Right now."

"No," he says, "what they need is for you to get in here and translate for me."

Master, gasps the marshman at my elbow, *help me*.

The face is thick with edema, but I can still recognize my canoe boy.

Chigger, I say, *why have they brought you here?*

He starts to answer, but is overcome by a coughing jag. His breath smells like charred meat. His lungs are finished. He won't live through the night.

Reiff rushes over with the torch. "Good man!" he says. "Keep him talking. Ask him about their command structure. No, belay that—ask him what they're planning to hit next."

I look up in amazement and say, "Go fuck yourself."

He squats to confront me. The torch hisses by my ear. "You do not want to go down that road, my friend," he says.

"The marshmen have a word for someone like you," I say. "*Unclean.*"

Reiff's eyes narrow; he still hasn't learned that supremely shameful word. He drives a rigid finger into my chest and bellows, "Out!" before turning his attention back to Chigger.

I pretend to walk calmly away. Then I free my sidearm.

But unlike the soldiers I'm used to, Reiff is a professional. The warm rubber grip is the last thing I feel before the ground leaps to my cheek.

I come to in the ward. My ears won't stop ringing; each heartbeat is a fresh blow to my head. I cover my eyes against the light of the bedside candle.

It's night. The ward is empty, save for Paul, who sits by me, whittling a reed with his homemade knife. I'm parched, but just as I start to ask for water, Paul gets up and races out to the hall.

I explore the back of my head with tentative fingers. There's a decent gash, and the hair all around is matted with blood. The fact that the wound hasn't even been laved is a puzzle that occupies my whirling mind.

The door flies open. *Ah, my water*, I croak.

Curtis steps into the room, looking taller and leaner than ever. The shine on his freshly shaven face seems to match his polished boots. He smells strongly of horses and cologne.

Paul scurries in after him, brandishing his homemade dirk.

Curtis rests a hand on the boy's head, then asks if he can have a look at the knife. Paul hands it over.

May I keep it for a while? Curtis asks.

Not too long! the boy says. Then he blushes, realizing he has just dictated terms to the general.

Don't worry, Curtis says. *I'll give it back*. He flips the boy a coin. Paul pockets it, then gently closes the door behind him.

"A good kid," Curtis says, brushing reed shavings from the chair. He admires Paul's knife for a moment before sitting down. "This is what a child of the marshes makes out of garbage," he says.

With a smooth and easy motion, he hurls the knife at a bed-post across the room. It bites into the wood with a loud *thunk*. "Well balanced, too," he says.

"Where are my patients?"

He waves off the question as he turns to me. "Part of this is my fault," he says. "I vouched for you. I didn't want to believe the reports. I had no idea you were so far gone."

"You're wrong about the pipeline," I say. "These are poor people. This time of year, there's always a shortage of cooking fuel."

"Administrator!" he says. The word hangs in the air for a moment between us, vibrating with disgust. "You pulled a weapon on Reiff."

"He was about to torture a child."

"A child? What you don't know about the enemy could fill an encyclopedia."

"On the contrary," I say. "He's sitting with me right now." And then it's so quiet between us that I can hear the faint suckling of the candle.

"Well," he says, "it's over. In a few weeks, the last of the new levees will be done, and then we'll pull the plug on these swamps, once and for all."

"You're draining the marshes?"

"Whoever controls the water, controls the marshman. I think you told me that once. No? It sounds like you, anyway."

"Quick, give me the bowl," I say. While I'm retching, a woman comes in with a pitcher. Curtis tells her to hurry up and leave, but she lingers by the bed.

This is the general? she asks. I recognize the voice. It's the laundress.

Curtis answers for himself. *I am the general*, he says.

Good, she says. *Here's what I bought with your money.*

She points awkwardly at his belly and fires before either of us can stop her. It's an old service revolver, drawn from beneath her robe. The impact throws his chair backward and lands him in a heap on the floor. "Fuck!" he cries. "What the fuck?"

She pulls the trigger again, but the action has jammed. She drops the gun and looks around the room, her eyes wide with the fear of not finishing. When she spots the homemade knife, the relief is evident.

Curtis tries to unstrap his sidearm, but his fingers are slippery with blood and the legs of the chair interfere. He turns to me and says, "Get my gun." Blood spurts from his abdominal aorta. "Get it," he says, his words starting to slur.

I kneel down and pull it free.

"Shoot," he gasps. But instead I toss it away.

There's shouting at the door. Someone pounds it with the butt of a rifle.

The laundress walks up to him and places her foot on his gut, right where the bullet went in. She leans into it, adding her weight bit by bit as Curtis's eyes roll back.

She turns and offers me the knife. I don't take it; nor do I move to stop her.

She digs her fingers into his hair. She's just touching the blade to his throat when the soldiers break through the door. One of them races over, slipping in the growing pool of blood. He's very capable, though. Without fully regaining his balance, he manages to shoot her cleanly through the forehead.

I slowly raise my hands as more soldiers pour into the room. Curtis is deathly pale. He lifts a dripping finger and manages one final word. Every head turns to me.

"Traitor."

(ELEVEN YEARS EARLIER)

1

Gus had been waiting in the café by the western gate for nearly two hours. He checked his watch to make sure it was set to local time. But of course it was. He'd changed it on the deck of the hospital ship. Officers were supposed to stay on fleet time, but months of boredom had put him in a defiant mood. He'd taken great pleasure turning back the hands for shore leave. The watch was correct; the boy was simply late.

He ordered another cup of the sweet sludge that passed for coffee in the port city and buried himself in his phrase book, a poor crumbling thing he'd rescued from a bin behind his college library.

He stared at the coffee when it came, weighing whether or not to mention the insect wing that winked at him from the settling foam. After a while, he turned to the waiter, who was reading a newspaper at the counter, and tried out one of his favorite marsh idioms.

Often the river will swallow a man's plans, he said, adding the marshman's characteristic shrug for emphasis. At least he hoped it was characteristic. He'd seen it often enough in old movies.

The waiter, a native of some kind but apparently not a marshman, folded his newspaper with an angry flourish and said, "We don't speak pidgin here."

Gus smiled apologetically and asked for the bill. He felt

foolish for assuming the waiter was a marshman. The port city was known as a melting pot, but the liberation of the marshes had polarized the locals into winners and losers. Perhaps the waiter's tribe was among the losers.

He made sure to leave a large tip, giving the foreign bills a sharp rap with his knuckles as if money were somehow to blame for the misunderstanding. Then he slipped past the waiter and abandoned the café.

The real heat of the day had begun. The cobblestones glowed under a veil of dust. Gus decided to return to his hotel in case the boy had left word for him there. He tried not to look defeated as he quit the old city. He'd been told that pickpockets could sense when things had turned against a tourist. That's when they liked to pounce.

He was dripping when he got back to the hotel, which was halfway up the escarpment that curved around the port like a copper bowl. His room wasn't large, but there was a fine bathtub with gilded feet, a relic of a previous occupation. The tub was the room's main attraction. That, and the view of the twin forts that guarded the straits of the bay.

After a cool bath, Gus sat on the balcony and worked a crossword. A maid brought him a clay pitcher covered with gauze. He hadn't ordered it, but he accepted the pitcher with another marsh idiom. *Where there is kindness*, he said, *no land is foreign*. His words seemed to frighten the girl, who ran off before he could pull out his wallet.

The drink was warm and salty, with a hint of a bitter fruit he couldn't identify. But despite the unpleasant taste, a glass of it quenched his thirst.

There wasn't much to do until the boy turned up. An excursion to the marshes was out of the question without a guide. Gus had planned to give him something extra if the tour was halfway decent, but even as he fantasized about lecturing the boy for being late, he knew he wouldn't deny him a tidy bonus. He was loath to punish a young person trying to lift himself up, especially here, in such a troubled corner of the world.

A goat appeared below the balcony and picked its way to the edge of the cliff, where it stopped to rub against a young palm tree, its pot-metal bell tolling rhythmically in the morning air.

Gus usually enjoyed a good crossword, but his eyes kept wandering down to the bay. The fleet was a series of smudges on the horizon maneuvering in and out of the haze. His hospital ship was out there somewhere, its pristine wards lined with empty beds.

He'd hoped to treat some marshmen, if only for bragging rights back home, but that hadn't materialized. Hostilities were over long before he arrived—not that there were many casualties to begin with. The campaign had been prosecuted entirely by marshmen under the supervision of a handful of military advisers. The warlord's troops had simply melted back across the northern border.

An air horn sang out in the harbor, two staccato notes followed by a long dolorous blast. Other horns joined in. Fishing dhows came and went, their sails never seeming to fill. Gus was surprised there was still fishing so late in the morning. Then again, what did he know about the local catch? He smiled at his presumption. There was guilty pleasure in knowing so little about a place.

He was beginning to think about lunch when a pack of noisy children drifted down from the parking lot. The youngest ones wore split loincloths or nothing at all. The rest were rowdy and hungry-looking—"feral" was the word that came to mind. They chased away the goat, then huddled at the base of the little tree and drew lots. The winner was a light-skinned girl in a pink dress whose hair was neatly braided. She was older than the others, and there was a quiet superiority about her that seemed to belong to the world of the hotel. Gus wondered if her parents were watching from another balcony.

She made a ceremony of taking off her sandals and arranging them on a rock. Then she reached under her dress and from a hidden fold produced a scrap of corrugated tin, a dangerous-looking thing the size and shape of a pocket comb. She put the scrap between her lips, wrapped her arms and legs around the tree, and started to climb, her dress filling with the hot breeze that rose from the harbor.

The tree flexed under her meager weight, its fronds shuddering each time she set her thighs. The higher she climbed, the more it bent toward the cliff's edge. Soon the girl was bobbing over a steep drop. A hawk patrolled the emptiness far below the pale soles of her feet. Gus felt the urge to call out, *Be careful!* Instead, he reached for his camera.

She parted the fronds when she got to the top, isolating a small green fruit, then set about cutting it loose. She sawed the stem with hypnotic steadiness, stopping only to wipe the sweat from her brow. She was at it a long time. The other children lost interest and drifted away in twos and threes. One of the boys made off with her sandals, then thought the better of it and silently returned them.

Gus switched to a longer lens, the better to flatten the dramatic seascape behind her. This was his favorite kind of composition: a native at an unfamiliar task, framed by a suitably exotic backdrop.

The focus ring on the lens was loose. His equipment was secondhand, the best he could afford on a junior officer's salary. Resolving the girl's elegant silhouette took longer than it should have. Just as he was about to snap the picture, the blade slipped from her hand and tumbled away. A magician's rose seemed to blossom in her palm.

She cried out, but it was more a cry of disgust than pain. Gus abandoned his camera and ran down to help. She was still high in the tree when he got to her. He told her to come down, first in in his own language, and then, when she showed no sign of understanding, in the marsh tongue.

She nodded, but kept twisting the fruit with her good hand to weaken the stem, yanking at it until it finally gave.

She took her time getting down, cradling the fruit like a favorite doll. The trunk of the tree was smeared with blood, but the fruit was unstained. Why she took such care to protect it was just one of the many questions Gus wanted to ask. Instead, he focused on her wound.

May I? he asked.

The girl nodded and extended her hand. Her shrewd brown eyes seemed to mock him, but he didn't care. Here he was, at last, treating a child of the marshes!

She needed stitches. *Come with me*, he said.

The girl hesitated. He thought she might want help carrying the fruit, but in trying to take it, he inadvertently smudged the husk with blood.

She snatched the fruit and hurled it away. Gus watched it skip down the rocks, bouncing ever higher until it burst. This was a setback. He'd been hoping to get her to talk about the fruit while he stitched her up. Instead, he resolved to ask about the charm she wore on her neck, an ancient ceramic token set in a heavy band of silver. Perhaps she'd even be persuaded to sell it.

A foreigner's hotel room interested the girl less than he would have imagined. She wasn't even curious about his doctor's bag, which he'd brought along for emergencies. He sat her on the bed, lined the bedside table with a clean towel, and laved the hand with bottled water. The cut was deep, but the blade had missed the tendons.

He prepared a shot of anesthetic. He was discreet about it;

nevertheless, she shrank from the syringe. *This will help*, he said. Her refusal was adamant, so he gave her stitches without it.

She bore them stoically. Gus was worried that her cries might draw the wrong kind of attention, but she didn't cry out, even when the suturing needle bit deep in the flesh. At first he kept up a reassuring patter, but she didn't want it. Her face was rigid with concentration.

Afterward, she was thirsty. He poured her glass after glass of the salty drink until the pitcher was empty.

More? he asked.

She shook her head. Then she went to the big bathtub and started filling it.

No, he said, turning off the water. It was one thing to stitch a girl's hand in his room, but something else to let her undress there. *Your hand needs to stay dry.*

She started filling the tub again, this time warning him off with her eyes.

In the end, Gus sat outside in the hallway while she had her bath. He left the door ajar in case someone came. Every time he heard a splash he called out, *Keep it dry!*, which she mimicked back at him.

Of course, she might have been saying something else. The marsh tongue didn't really sound the way it looked in the pages of a book.

After the bath, she appeared at the door, her braids dripping all over the pink dress. She led him away from the room with a certain urgency, as if she were suddenly nervous about being discovered inside the hotel. And, in fact, as they crossed the lobby, the clerk rose from his wicker stool and began to berate her. She answered with an imperious toss of her chin.

When they were outside, Gus realized he'd left his camera. He turned back for it, but she grabbed his sleeve and pulled him away from the hotel. He didn't really resist. From time to time he even closed his eyes against the glare and let himself be led. He'd started the morning as a tourist, but now he was something more: a physician with his patient. Surely that conferred a kind of protection, even in the port city.

They walked down the driveway and out onto the road, where they were soon overtaken by an old hansom loaded with sacks of grain. The girl called to the driver, who climbed down from the spring board to help her in. Gus tried to squeeze in among the sacks, too, but there wasn't room. He was willing to sit up top, but the girl barked instructions, and the driver set to work heaving his bulky cargo to the side of the road. When Gus was finally settled, the poor dripping man climbed back up, touched the nag's ribs with his whip, and the carriage lurched forward.

The girl stared out her hazy window as they rode. She'd chosen the side with the view of the harbor. Gus's window, on the other hand, gave out on the cut strata of the hill. He asked where they were going, but all she said was, *You'll see.* He called up through the hatch, but the driver didn't answer.

The silence was irritating. Gus didn't like being considered superfluous, but he told himself to relax. He would have been more comfortable in uniform, but at least his eyes were open, and his wallet full.

After a while, the driver's hand appeared with two bananas. The girl gave them to Gus. He peeled one and started eating, but she stared at him until he offered to peel hers, too.

Is the pain very bad? he asked.

The girl shrugged. It seemed she was simply used to having her fruit peeled by others.

They came to a halt at the fortified gates of a private compound. The carriage rocked as two armed men climbed aboard, one on each side of the driver. Then the gates parted, and they rolled into a dusty courtyard, where a handsome marshman with a crooked nose and a carefully trimmed beard waved the carriage to a halt. Gus noticed that the cord around his headscarf was purple. All the other cords he'd seen were black. Then again, virtually all of his exposure to marshmen had been in the form of black-and-white gravures in the pages of his father's moldering travel magazines.

The girl leaped from the carriage, flung herself into the marshman's arms, and pressed his hand to her cheek. He was very tender with her. Gus liked the way he swept back her braids as he knelt to inspect her wound.

The marshman rewrapped the bandage and dismissed the girl. Then he turned to Gus and said, "You sewed it well."

"She was incredibly brave," Gus said. "She wouldn't let me numb it."

"She's always been afraid of syringes," the marshman said, but Gus could tell he was pleased with the compliment. "You're with the fleet?"

Gus nodded.

"By the way, my daughter thinks you're a spy. She says you take too many pictures."

"I wish I were a spy," Gus said. "It would make me a lot more interesting."

The marshman smiled. His teeth were full of gold. "Yes, I can see why she likes you."

"Does she?"

"She wouldn't have brought you here if she didn't." The marshman extended his hand. "I am the Magheed," he said. "My daughter Thali and I are grateful for your attention. You should know that she speaks your language perfectly well. Her mother was a native of your country."

Gus introduced himself, then bowed and said, *Let us rather be strangers than friends.*

The Magheed laughed and corrected the saying, which Gus had gotten backward. "I like this one," he said, turning to his men. "Even if he *is* a spy."

The other marshmen smiled uncomfortably.

"Tonight you eat with us," the Magheed said.

"That's very kind," Gus said, "but I have other plans. I hired a guide to show me the ruins."

"A tour of the marshes? So late in the day?"

"My guide seems to have vanished."

"You paid him a deposit?"

Gus nodded.

"How much?"

The Magheed winced when Gus told him the figure. "Unfortunately," he said, "you hired a scoundrel. What did he look like?"

The Magheed called over one of his retainers and translated as Gus described the boy. "We'll find him," the Magheed said. "Meanwhile, I'll send a man to the hotel for your things."

Gus spent a pleasant afternoon exploring the Magheed's compound. Thali was never far away. She'd changed into a robe and headscarf that made her look like a classic marsh girl. She followed him, ducking behind a gnarled cedar or a whitewashed wall whenever he turned around, but never completely out of sight.

Eventually he made his way down to the beach and took off his shoes, the better to enjoy the fine pink sand. There was a promising breaker twenty meters offshore that looked perfect for surf-casting. Gus wished he had a rod and some tackle. He would have liked to present his host with a fresh fish, even if it was pulled from his own waters.

Thali watched from behind an overturned dory as he walked out on the jetty. When he reached the end of the rocks, he dangled his feet in the fabled waters of the bay. The water was full of jellyfish; the sun was unrelenting. He stayed longer than he wanted to. It seemed incumbent on him to prove that foreigners weren't weak.

She was gone when he got down from the jetty, but she'd laid out a blanket for him in the shade of the dory. There was a tray with almonds and grapes, and a darkening clay pitcher of the same strange drink he'd had at the hotel. He ate a few grapes, which were small and quite sour, then closed his eyes for a while and dozed.

He mistook the call to dinner for a call to prayer, and wound up being late to table, but the Magheed greeted him in high spirits. Throughout the meal, he kept hinting at a special treat.

When an enormous flatfish cooked in a sarcophagus of salt was served, to much applause, Gus was given the honor of cracking it open with a huge iron spoon. The Magheed offered him the choice portion: the cheeks.

The fish was delicious, and Gus thanked his host profusely, but the Magheed's eyes were still merry. "Just wait," he said.

At the end of the meal, a bowl of scented water was passed around the table. Gus dipped his fingers like everyone else. The Magheed was the last to dip his fingers. People clapped when he dried them, and Gus thought the evening was concluded.

But then two marshmen came in dragging a hooded boy who was cursing and struggling. At the Magheed's signal, one of the men struck him behind the knees with the butt of a rifle. The boy fell to the floor. This happened directly in front of Gus.

The Magheed unhooded him, then turned to Gus and asked, "Is this the one?"

The boy's face was bloody and one of his eyes was swollen shut, but Gus recognized his young guide. "I'm sure there's an explanation," he said.

The Magheed smiled ironically. "Of course there is. This little thief wanted your money."

The boy burst into tears. The Magheed grabbed him by the hair. "You never meant to give this man a tour, did you?" he said.

The boy pleaded with Gus. He said his mother had started coughing blood during the night and begged him to stay with her. He'd tried to leave a message with the waiter at the café, but the man refused to talk to him.

"It's true!" Gus said. "The waiter at that café doesn't like the marsh tongue."

The Magheed yanked the boy's hair. "By stealing from my guest, you have stolen from me."

The boy began to blubber. "I didn't steal," he cried. "I didn't."

The Magheed showed Gus the rifle the guard had used as a bludgeon. "This is a very expensive cape gun," he said. "I spoke with the dealer who sold it to the boy this morning."

"Why would he go and buy a gun?"

"Why wouldn't he?" the Magheed said, handing the cape gun to Gus. "It's yours now."

Gus didn't want to accept the gun, but the Magheed leaned it against the table next to him. "Take it," he said. "It's custom-made. Good quality."

Then he squatted next to the boy and spoke softly in his ear. "Tell my guest what we do to thieves."

"I'm not a thief," the boy whimpered.

"I like the gun," Gus said. "Let's call it even."

"I wish we could," the Magheed said, replacing the boy's hood. The boy resisted, but the guards held him tight.

The Magheed unsheathed his dirk. He raised his voice and said, "A thief in the marshes forfeits his hand."

The boy started to choke inside the hood.

Bare his arm, the Magheed said.

One of the guards knelt by the boy, slid back his sleeve, and pinned the arm to the floor.

Gus leaped to his feet. "Please!" he cried. "No!"

The Magheed winked at Gus and held his finger to his lips. He took the iron spoon from the fish plate and raised it over the boy's wrist, then motioned to the guard. The guard silently readied a truncheon behind the boy's head. *Get ready with napkins*, the Magheed said. *There's going to be a lot of blood.*

Then, in one swift motion, he brought the spoon down on the boy's wrist. At the same instant, the guard clubbed the boy's head. He went limp.

The table erupted in laughter, but Gus felt sick. "Thank God," he said. "Thank God. I thought you were really going to do it."

"We're not barbarians," the Magheed said. He nodded to the guard, who drew a wicked little knife, lifted the boy's wrist, and in one fluid motion made a shallow incision all the way around.

"When he wakes up," the Magheed said, "he'll be told that his hand was indeed removed, but you insisted on sewing it back. You'll be famous. Tales of your mercy will precede you. Now, as for your tour, anyone in the street could have told you that the marshes are closed."

"Closed? I didn't know," Gus said. Actually, he'd heard something to that effect, but he'd also been told that access to the ruins was routine, a matter of a few simple bribes.

"Not to worry," the Magheed said. "You'll have your tour. I'll see to it myself."

2

The Magheed's party quit the port city the next day. Gus had hoped to send his parents a cable to the effect that he was being dragged into the marshes by a band of friendly natives, but there wasn't time. If only his father could see him now, barreling along on a flatbed truck with the Magheed's men, their long black robes chattering in the wind!

After clearing the city gates, the caravan rolled unchallenged across trackless scrubland, trailing the marshmen's songs and laughter. The so-called closure of the marshes hardly posed a problem. Most of the checkpoints were shuttered. The few that were open were manned by local militia who took pains to seek out the Magheed and pay their respects.

There was plenty of trading along the way. At each stop, as crates were tossed down from idling trucks and others heaved up and secured, Gus was served food and water in Bakelite bowls from an old picnic set. The other men on the truck passed earthen jugs and baskets of fruit. He would have been happy to share in these communal meals, but was told that the Magheed's daughter had prepared his portion herself.

By late afternoon, as scrubland gave way to fertile ground, the caravan's wake no longer boiled with red dust. The ride began to set Gus's teeth on edge; the tires, which had been bled for traction in the sand, vibrated badly on hardpack. Through a slit in his borrowed headcloth, Gus watched for changes in the drainage ditch that paralleled the road. As the trucks rolled on, the bottom of the ditch grew dark and moist; then the velvety silt erupted in cordgrass, sedge, and cattails. By the end of the day, the ditch ran with water and was choked with phragmites, the typical reed of the marshes, arrayed in an endless picket that swayed as the caravan rumbled past.

When the road finally ended at the trucking dock of a dilapidated warehouse, the Magheed's party dismounted, filed through labyrinthine gates designed for livestock, then loaded onto several private barges. The boats were tethered in the final lock of a canal that stretched north into the darkness.

Being on the water made the marshmen easy. Once the baggage was secured, some shared silent cigarettes; others arranged themselves on pyramids of rolled rugs and dozed. The tang of goat stew wafted from the women's barge.

After everyone had fed, the decks were transformed into a patchwork of grass mats and heavy quilts. The Magheed descended from the towpath like a father coming to kiss his children good night.

Gus rose when the Magheed appeared beside his pallet. The Magheed embraced him and welcomed him to the marshes as if this were the first time they'd met. He asked if there was anything he could do to make the journey more pleasant. Gus thanked him and said that Thali was taking good care of him.

The Magheed's eyebrows rose in surprise, but then he turned and opened his arms to take in the high brick walls of the canal. "Built to accommodate the rainy season," he said, "but as you see, passable in the dry months, as well. Unlike the old canal."

"A fine piece of engineering."

"I asked for gunboats," the Magheed said, "and this is what I got instead. Thali thinks I should be more grateful. She tells me the canal represents progress."

"Doesn't it?"

"Perhaps," he said, "but for whom?"

•

The barges got under way in the night. Gus slept fitfully, his dreams fed by groaning beams, bullwhips, the burble of on-rushing water. He was woken in the foggy predawn by a small boy who tugged his sleeve and called him *Master*. After a breakfast of flatbread and yogurt, the boy led him up a ladder to the towpath, where a hunting party was convening.

Gus was approached by one of the Magheed's guards, a grizzled elder with a leather eye patch named Fennuk, who knelt and opened a soft rifle case. *Your weapon*, he said, presenting Gus with the cape gun that had been bought with his tour money, but not before burnishing it one last time with a chamois. Then he stood and gave Gus two pouches of ammunition—a gift, he emphasized, from his own pocket, not the Magheed's.

Open them, Fennuk said.

One of the pouches had rifle slugs; the other, cartridges of bird-shot. Gus hefted the pouches with an appreciative nod.

Ten of each, Fennuk said. He seemed put out that Gus hadn't bothered to count them.

Fennuk and the other marshmen of the Magheed's inner circle carried brand-new automatic rifles. Gus examined the markings on one of the barrels; the weapons had been manufactured in a suburb of the capital city, not far from where he grew up.

The marshmen shouldered their rifles when Gus walked by, assuming stern expressions and sometimes even offering salutes, which he reluctantly returned. The deference made him uncomfortable. Yes, he was an officer, an ambassador of the nation that had sent rifles, but hadn't his people also built the canal?

The foreign guns were for the Magheed's retinue, but every marshman had a weapon, although some of them were so thick with rust that Gus doubted they could be fired. Even the youngest member of the party, the little fellow called Hamza who'd woken Gus that morning, carried a reed slingshot. In fact, Hamza's slingshot was responsible for the day's first kill: a thrush the boy managed to shoot through the eye with a lead pellet.

A steady walking pace outstripped the barges. When the fog burned off, Gus was finally able to photograph the ancient alluvial plain he'd spent so many hours daydreaming about as a child: an Eden of reeds and silver waterways, where ruined Bronze Age palaces seemed to doze like exhausted parents, oblivious to the joyful birds that ran riot along their spines.

The marshmen waited patiently while Gus composed his pictures, but he felt guilty for slowing the hunt. He kept telling himself to put the camera away, and even managed to slip it back in its leather case a few times, but it never seemed to stay there long.

After nearly an hour of walking, someone gave a signal, and Gus was rushed up the towpath to a clearing, where space was made for him atop a crumbling clay wall.

Fennuk pointed out a disturbance in the grass at a hundred meters. *Wild pig*, he said.

Gus was handed a battered spotting scope whose optics flattened the animal into a tiny menacing silhouette. The pig was rooting in clumps of arrowgrass. Gus waited for someone to take a shot, but apparently that honor fell to him. Fennuk motioned for the marshmen to step aside, then fished a slug from one of Gus's pouches and pressed it into his hand.

Gus was willing, but there was a problem. He held up the cape gun and confessed that he didn't know how to open it.

Pursing his lips in disbelief, Fennuk worked the latch behind the barrels. The gun broke soundlessly. Gus tried to load the slug, but it was loose in the barrel, and the action wouldn't close. He wondered if Fennuk had given him slugs of the wrong caliber.

Fennuk exchanged puzzled glances with the other marshmen. He took the cape gun, pulled the slug from the left barrel, and slid it into the right barrel, where it fit perfectly. Then he took a bird-shot shell from Gus's other pouch and loaded the left barrel.

Bird-shot, left; slug, right, he said, closing the action and handing the gun back.

By the time the gun was loaded and Gus had taken a kneeling stance, the pig had moved farther off. Now it was a tiny blur in the V of the open sight. Gus doubted he could hit it from such a distance, but he lined up the shot; rested his finger on the trigger; took two deep breaths and held the third; then fired.

He wasn't prepared for the recoil, which knocked him over and somehow bloodied his nose. *A hit?* he asked. At this, the marshmen couldn't contain their laughter. Fennuk shook his head. *Wrong trigger*, he said.

Gus had fired bird-shot instead of the slug.

The shot startled the pig, but didn't spook it. Instead, it turned to the noise, twisting its huge head and snorting.

As if to prove there was nothing wrong with the gun, Fennuk took it from Gus, swung it to his shoulder, and quickly fired.

The marshman with the spotting scope raised his hand and whooped. The party fanned into the swamp grass, the young men racing ahead, the older ones chatting excitedly. Fennuk brought up the rear with a confident unhurried gait.

Gus supposed he was embarrassed, but he was happy for Fennuk and thrilled with the sight of the marshmen celebrating around the fallen pig, which made for some excellent pictures.

When the barges finally caught up with the hunting party, most of the men climbed down to the decks to rest. Gus stayed on the towpath, where there was at least a breath of wind. Fennuk made a place for him in the shade of a defunct tollhouse and offered him boiled water from a canteen. For once, Gus was happy to be singled out for special treatment. The typical solution for a marshman's thirst was a leather bag dipped in the canal.

Fennuk squatted by him in the shade. After Gus had drunk

his fill, Fennuk fixed him with his good eye. *Did you like the ammunition?* he asked.

Very much, Gus said.

There was a long silence between them. Somewhere, a mule driver laid into his animal with a whip.

They say you're a doctor, Fennuk said.

Gus nodded.

Fennuk turned and stripped off his tunic, revealing an angry carbuncle between his shoulder blades.

Gus examined the carbuncle. *Use a warm wet cloth*, he said. *Let it sit.*

Fennuk pulled his dirk and mimed heating it, then using it as a lance. *Like that*, he said. *Fast.*

Gus shook his head. *Fast is risky.*

Fennuk gave a thumbs-up and said, "Yes, okay!" The foreign words sounded false on his tongue.

All right, Gus said. *But I'll need my bag.*

Fennuk grinned and said he'd already sent Hamza to fetch it.

Word got out that the foreign doctor was willing to treat marshmen. In the two days it took to reach the end of the canal, Gus was very busy. The health of the marshmen was generally good. Their teeth suffered from the grit in their diet, and there were many cases of poor vision caused by river parasites, but the difficulty of life in the marshes, coupled with a healthy if monotonous diet, made for vigorous men.

Nearly a dozen youngsters presented botched circumcisions, weeping infections that were traceable to an itinerant barber, apparently the only man in the northern marshes who circumcised.

Gus took his concerns to the Magheed. "The man's a butcher," Gus said. "His dressings are filthy."

The Magheed sighed. "Yes, he's a charlatan, but we lost most of the good barbers to the war. We can't stop our boys from going to him. An uncircumcised marshman can't marry."

"It's a simple procedure. I'd be happy to do it—with your permission, of course. I'd just need some supplies."

"Supplies aren't a problem," the Magheed said. "Let's talk about your fee."

"My fee? Well, you could teach me how to shoot that damned cape gun."

The Magheed laughed. "Teach a spy to shoot?" he said. "You drive a hard bargain." Then he embraced Gus, pressing a rough palm to the back of his neck, and said, "Thank you. It's not easy to find a doctor who will treat marshmen."

"You'd be surprised," Gus said. "My friends in the fleet are all big believers in this mission. Your neighbor to the north had no business in the marshes."

"That's true. He was a threat to your interests as well. An enemy of free trade. You know our saying, *The enemy of my enemy is my friend*?"

But Gus wanted the Magheed to understand just how deep his feelings ran. "It's not just that," he said. "This is a beautiful place—an important place. I came because I wanted to help."

The Magheed nodded sympathetically. "Thali was right about you," he said. "You're an idealist. I like idealists, but they don't last very long out here. Sometimes, I wish I was one myself."

At the end of the canal, where a tributary of the ancient river lapped the concrete of a new dike, the Magheed's party changed to smaller, river-going barges made of bundled reeds. Gus was looking forward to climbing onto one of those picturesque boats, but the Magheed had other plans.

"You're with me," he said. He led Gus to a landing where a long black chief's canoe lay grounded in the shadow of the reeds.

Gus was elated. He'd tacked an antique postcard of just such a boat over his childhood bed; when his mother finally threw the card away, on the grounds that it was filling his sheets with inky crumbs, he'd sulked for a week.

He put his shoulder to the heavy canoe side by side with the Magheed's men. It was awkward on land but rode surprisingly high on the water, its sharp keel parting the red algae like a knife.

"A full day's journey," the Magheed said, as the prow swung into the current. "Take all the pictures you like, but keep your head down. For some unhappy souls, the war will never be over."

The banks of the waterway were thick with giant reeds whose tips met overhead, creating long, creaking arcades. Gus was grateful for the shade, and he admired the way the shifting grasses filtered the light, but after several hours of claustrophobic progress, it was a relief when the tall grass finally fell away, revealing a vast brackish lake.

The paddlers did their best to hug the shore, but there were long stretches of open water. As the sun fell, a stiff wind kicked up from the west. Whitecaps broke across the gunwales. Hamza was in constant motion, bailing with a huge wooden scoop. Fennuk beat a punishing pace on a skin drum; the paddlers, who'd kept rhythm earlier in the day with spirited singing, fell silent, their backs running with sweat.

Gus had weathered storms with the fleet, but never in an open boat, right down in violent water. The Magheed, sensing his discomfort, pointed out a faint glow on the horizon and shouted over the wind, "Nearly there!" Fennuk saw it, too, and promptly fired a few rounds into the air. The paddlers cheered when the shots were answered. Then Hamza started a new song, which carried them all the way to shore.

•

Gus didn't remember much of that night beyond staggering onto a beach and being led to a bunk. He said he was too tired to eat, but the truth was that he was seasick from the rough crossing. He buried himself in blankets and slept.

In the morning, Hamza was waiting at his door with a tray. While Gus tore into a stack of flatbread, the boy explained that everyone else had gone fishing for barbel. There'd been a great run of them. Barbel were good to eat smoked; they were delicious with rice; you could practically scoop them out of the water with your hand.

Gus felt bad for the little fellow. He offered Hamza the rest of his flatbread and told him to go join the fishing party, but the boy said it was impossible. So, with Hamza moping at his heels, Gus gave himself a tour of the Magheed's village, starting with the building where he'd spent the night: an old granary that had been converted into a clinic. Gus had slept in the surgeon's apartment, which was furnished with sturdy reed furniture and good insect netting. The one false note was the creaking old boxspring. Gus had woken several times in the night wishing for a simple pallet of grass.

The examining room was dusty from disuse, but well fitted with a porcelain operating table and a matching cabinet full of fresh, military-grade supplies. There was no lock on the cabinet, which Gus took as a sign of the Magheed's absolute authority in the village. There was a decent surgical lamp, a bench with an electric burner, and an old-fashioned stovetop autoclave.

Hamza took him out back and proudly showed off the clinic's generator, which sat on a skid stenciled with the words PROTECTIVE SERVICES.

The only other generator in the village was at the Magheed's house, a modest brick bungalow identical to the countless tax houses Gus had seen along the canal, with one exception: a wall of ornate foreign windows facing the lake.

They wandered down to the beach, where the chief's canoe

lay drying in the sun. The lagoon was too bright for pictures, which was a shame; its surface was a flawless mirror of clouds and beating wings. Judging from the herons stalking hundreds of meters offshore, the lake was scarcely deeper than a wading pool. Gus felt foolish for having been so scared during the crossing.

Beyond the lagoon, at the edge of a barren mud flat, was a brickyard. The kiln was huge and conical. Its glowing peak belched smoke. Hamza told him that in the dry season it was fired for weeks on end. Gus marveled at the genius of the design: by day, the kiln was for cooking bricks; by night, it was a beacon for storm-tossed boats.

The highlight of the tour was the reed guesthouse. Gus had seen pictures of guesthouses, but pictures didn't do justice to the soaring arched ceiling, or the sense one felt, standing just inside the doorway, of being in the belly of an antediluvian beast. The structural ribs were so well bound they looked mono-lithic, the individual reeds having been compressed into a smooth mass like ivory. The hanging brass lanterns were brightly pol-ished; the hearth neatly raked. The rugs that lined the floor wouldn't have looked out of place in an admiral's quarters.

Gus wasn't sure he was welcome, so he stood back until Hamza pushed him in and marched him over to the hearth, where a toothless old man was grinding beans.

Coffee, Hamza said.

The man nodded and started banking the coals as if the order had come from the Magheed himself.

When the barges arrived that night, the return to the village was marked with a great feast. The centerpiece of the meal, borne by four strapping marshmen, was a gigantic platter of rice topped with a whole roasted calf. Gus was among the first served. He was installed in a place of honor with the Magheed's inner circle; the villagers, on the other hand, cycled through the guesthouse in successive seatings. It was many hours before the last marshman was fed.

Afterward, the Magheed walked him back to the clinic. "Tell me," he said, "when do you have to report back to the fleet?"

"In five days, I'm afraid."

"If it could be arranged, would you like to stay longer?"

"Absolutely."

"In that case," the Magheed said, "leave it to me."

3

Gus found it hard to believe that a marshman could influence fleet deployments, but two days later, Hamza woke him from a deep sleep, whispering, *Master, a foreign soldier is here.*

Gus dressed quickly, grabbed his bag, and followed the boy to one of the long communal stables near the brickyard. It was an hour or so before dawn. Mist overhung the lake, but the air in the village was cool and dry. A front had blown through during the night.

In his rush out the door, Gus had draped a thick headcloth over his shoulders like a cape, but the chill cut right through it. The odor of smoldering dung from the kiln mingled with the funk of rising water. Someone was cursing a buffalo for giving poor milk. Cries of migrating geese echoed across the lake.

The soldier was waiting for him at the stables, leaning against the arched doorway. He was dressed as a marshman, with a rough-spun tunic, a checkered white headcloth, and a rifle slung over his shoulder. He had the lanky build of a marshman, as well, but he was too tall for a native, and his tangled beard was too light. He was smoking an acrid local cigarette. There clearly wasn't much pleasure in it.

"Major Curtis," he said. "Protective Services."

Gus was suddenly aware of his appearance. He regretted the headcloth on his shoulders, which seemed to suggest that he didn't know how it was meant to be worn.

Curtis led Gus into the depths of the stables, where a young marshman was writhing on a blanket. His hands were bound behind his back. A filthy hood stifled his moans.

"This might be easier at the clinic," Gus said.

Curtis shook his head.

"How about some light, then?" Gus said.

"Not yet. He doesn't see your face."

Gus dug into his bag for a surgical mask; Curtis covered up with two expert winds of his headcloth.

"Okay," Curtis said, training a flashlight on the marshman while Gus removed the hood. The light made the prisoner flinch. His left eye was grotesquely swollen. His cheeks shone with fluid.

A rag had been stuffed in his mouth. Gus pulled it out as gently as he could, but even so, the bad eye quivered like a shirred egg.

"It's been like that for a couple of days," Curtis said. "Can you save it?"

Gus examined it briefly. "No. How did it happen?"

"We caught him with a crate of stolen assault rifles," Curtis said. Gus waited for more, but Curtis didn't elaborate.

Gus propped the marshman's neck with the folded head-cloth. At first the man resisted, but Gus whispered some calming words. At the sound of them, the marshman's good eye filled with tears.

"I'll leave you lovebirds alone," Curtis said.

A drink of water revived the marshman. Gus continued his examination by flashlight. In addition to the ruined eye, there was a suppurating ring of lacerations across the man's brow and around the back of his head.

Gus asked the marshman how he'd gotten into such trouble.

The marshman wept. He said he was a fisherman, not a smuggler. He was moving the rifles for a cousin. The foreign soldiers ambushed him at one of the locks of the canal. They yelled at him and made him kneel, then wrapped barbed wire around his head and pulled it tight to get him to talk. One time, a metal splinter got in his eye. The pain of the splinter was worse than anything. They refused to let him pluck it.

What did they want to know? Gus asked.

Where to find my cousin.

Tell me now, Gus said. *It's not too late. I can help.*

The marshman went silent.

In the interest of sparing the man another interrogation, Gus gave himself permission to tell a white lie. *The punishment for moving rifles*, he said, *is the same as for stealing them.* To emphasize the point, Gus reached around him and squeezed one of his wrists.

The marshman started shaking violently. Finally, he spoke. *His name is Jahaish. He's hiding with his in-laws, who sell smoked fish out of a houseboat on the lake.*

The betrayal drained the tension from his body. He began pleading with Gus. *I told you everything*, he said. *Now save my eye. I know you can.*

Gus told him it couldn't be saved.

The marshman was prepared to hear that. He cried harder, but there was a new calculation behind his weeping.

Curtis came back in. "Good," he said. "You got him talking."

Gus told him what the marshman had said, then added, "He wants to be paid for the eye."

"Sounds about right. Can he travel?"

"No, it needs to come out. Those lacerations on his head need some attention, too."

"Fine," Curtis said. "Just don't give him anything that'll make him sleep. I need him awake. Also, I could use some breakfast."

"There's food at the guesthouse," Gus said.

"I mean real-people food. Can your boy cook me some eggs?"

Gus shook his head.

"Anyway, come find me after you fix him up. You and I need to have a little chat."

•

Gus could have gotten by with a local, but he gave the fisherman a mild sedative to make the procedure easier on both of them. The eye came out cleanly. He was curious about the splinter but left the eye intact. He'd read that marshmen liked to bury their flesh in the family plot, so he wrapped the eye in wax paper and tucked it in the empty wallet that hung around the fisherman's neck.

After washing up, Gus left his patient sleeping on the table and stepped outside. He lingered on the stoop, taking in the fresh air. It was a great relief. The fisherman stank, and the windows had been shut tight against a gritty breeze.

A table had been set for Curtis in the shade of a nearby acacia tree. He was just finishing breakfast. "Look what your marshmen did to me," he said, dropping a bright yellow biscuit onto his plate. The tin plate rang out like a cymbal.

"That's pollen cake," Gus said. "It takes forever to gather pollen from the reeds. You should feel honored."

"Is my guy ready to go?"

"As a matter of fact, he's sleeping."

"I told you not to do that," Curtis said.

"Judgment call. Those wounds on his head were worse than I thought. He said something about being interrogated with a wire."

"The locals call it the *liar's headband*. We only use it on hard cases."

"He didn't seem like such a hard case."

"Maybe that's because we used it on him."

"Does the Magheed know about this?"

Curtis rapped a pack of cigarettes on the table, then fished one out and lit it. "Know about it? Who do you think these smugglers work for? I've been trying to nail that guy for months." Then he stood and wrapped his hands around the acacia's trunk, deftly avoiding the thorns, and leaned in, stretching his powerful calves. Even gaunt and exhausted, he was a handsome man. He wore his wind-whipped headscarf like a crown.

"Why would the Magheed steal guns? His men are well armed."

"To buy loyalty from the other chiefs. Gifts, bribes. Call it what you will. Do you really not know these things?"

"Enlighten me."

"No. You enlighten *me*. What's your outfit?"

"I'm with the fleet, but this isn't a posting. I'm a guest."

Curtis laughed. "Oh, a *guest*!"

"Aren't we all?"

Curtis took a long drag on his cigarette. "I don't expect you to understand what goes on out here. But I am short on language skills. My translator took a bullet in the neck two weeks ago. I could use someone who knows the lingo."

"And these people could use a doctor."

"They should have thought about that before they shot the last one. Here's the thing. Our footprint in the region is changing. I've been told to police up our ordnance—all of it, including the rifles. Do you suppose these marshmen are going to like having their teeth pulled?"

"Probably not," Gus said.

"Which is why I was against arming them in the first place." Curtis took a final drag, then crushed the cigarette with the toe of his boot. "What's your name, anyway?"

Gus told him. Curtis wrote it down, along with his rank and serial number.

"Well, you seem all right, Lieutenant, other than being a prick about the anesthesia. Welcome to the marshes."

"Thank you, sir."

"Don't thank me yet. This isn't a free ride. You're going to be my eyes and ears in this village. And you will translate for me as needed."

"Yes, sir."

"Whether or not you approve of my methods. Are we clear?"

"Crystal clear."

Curtis grabbed the pollen cake from his plate and tossed it to Gus. "Go ahead, go nuts," he said. "Nobody around here likes this stuff. They told you it was some big honor? My guess is they just wanted to watch you break your teeth."

By evening, Curtis had had enough of waiting for the fisherman to wake up. He strode into the clinic, fitted his prisoner with a hood, and declared him ready for travel. Gus helped him down to the lagoon, where Curtis's motorized launch bobbed in the shallows. The fisherman collapsed when they reached water's edge, so Curtis scooped him up and carried him like a bride to the boat, then bound his wrists and ankles to the cleats.

Gus was in the middle of explaining how to change the fisherman's dressings when Curtis tossed the bag of supplies back to him, saying, "Save this for someone who needs it." Then he produced a two-way radio from a duffel and pitched it to Gus. "I'm assuming you know how to use one of these," he said. As an afterthought, he unstrapped his sidearm and pitched it across, too. "And here's your signing bonus."

Gus's hands were full. He bobbled the gun, dropping it in the sand.

Curtis scowled. "Keep that weapon clean," he said. "You're going to need it." He yanked the starter cord, and the old engine burst to life in a cloud of blue smoke, startling a kingfisher that had swooped down for a feeding run. As he lowered the propeller into the water, Curtis shouted a final instruction: "You hear anything even remotely suspicious, use that radio!"

"I will!" Gus said.

The launch churned northward, leaving a trail of silver filigree on the lake. Gus stood at attention for a long time, enduring bites from invisible gnats. When the boat's silhouette finally melted into the horizon, he tucked the pistol into his waistband and covered the grip with the tail of his shirt. The radio was too big to fit in his pocket, so he palmed it and did his best to hide the rest with his forearm, the way his shipmates had taught him to move an illicit bottle of whiskey from deck to deck.

"You will, what?" Thali asked. She was standing just a few feet away in her willowy black robe, as if the lengthening shadows of the reeds had risen from the sand to greet him.

"Do my best," he said vaguely. "To help."

"Rest tonight," she said. "The clinic will be crowded tomorrow."

"Do you know where I could find your father?" Gus asked. "I wanted to thank him for letting me stay."

"He left a few hours ago to settle a dispute in one of his holdings."

"Did he say when he'll be back?"

Thali shrugged. "Don't worry," she said. "There'll be plenty of time to thank him later."

Gus's days soon fell into a rhythm. The clinic overflowed from early morning to midafternoon, when the crush of patients would cause the domed ceiling of the surgery to drip with condensation. In the worst heat of the day, there was the guesthouse, where he spent hours sitting very still, coffee cup in hand, listening to the quiet chatter of marshmen. He never tired of it, despite the seeming monotony of the topics: hunting; the depth of waterways; who had leased what tiny plot, and for how much.

The evenings were for writing letters, photography, or fishing. Every night, precisely at eight, Thali served him supper at the long marble table in her father's dining room, gossiping about the day's patients as he sipped the exceedingly weak gin and tonic that she insisted was good for his nerves.

Thali made the drink herself, like the true mistress of the house. She was older than Gus figured when he first saw her, perhaps fourteen or even fifteen, although she refused to say exactly how old. It didn't really matter. After a long day with patients, many of whom barely spoke to him out of deference, he was glad for the attention of a lively young girl. She was good company. Gus felt more at ease at that table than anywhere else in the village.

After two busy weeks without word from Curtis, Gus was beginning to think that his services as a translator wouldn't be needed after all. The only official communication he'd received was the letter notifying him of his transfer to the marshes.

Gus had plans for that letter. It would have pride of place on the wall of his office when he got back home. He already knew how he'd frame it: double-matted, with a cutout at the bottom for a photograph of cheerful marsh children gathered in a scrum; or perhaps a more personal one of him with the Magheed—if such a picture didn't violate any cultural sensitivities.

He put the letter in a manila folder and stored it in the strongbox by his bed, next to the sidearm and radio. He hadn't touched the radio since the night Curtis gave it to him, although he'd thought about using it once or twice. He kept it available, but not really at the ready, a reflection of his ambivalence about informing on patients. Trust was at the root of healing. A doctor was obliged to keep confidences, even here in a war zone.

On the other hand, as much as Gus admired the marshmen's fighting spirit, he didn't feel he could turn a blind eye to theft, especially the theft of weapons. One morning, he overheard something troubling while standing at the window of the surgery. Two young men he'd just circumcised were sitting nearby on the stone bench in the yard. Gus always made circumcisions wait at least an hour, to make sure there weren't any complications. The wait wasn't really a burden; in fact, a turn on the bench was quickly becoming a rite of passage.

Normally, there'd be high-spirited chatter from the boys on the bench, but these two, a pair of brothers from a village on the far shore of the lake, were being secretive. There'd been something not quite right about them from the start. They were shy to the point of rudeness, refusing to answer even basic questions about their health. Gus had had a hard time getting more out of them than their names—Kareem and Adnan—and the fact that they were apprentice boatbuilders. They'd insisted on paying, even after Gus explained there'd be no fee.

There was always the possibility that one of them was in pain and reluctant to ask for help, so Gus lingered by the window after loading the autoclave. A breeze rattled the acacia, obscuring some of the words, but even so, he was quite sure he heard Adnan, the elder brother, say, *At last, there will be a fountain of fire*, to which Kareem replied, *God willing!*

Then Adnan started sketching in the dirt with the stem of a cattail. *This*, he said, *is where you light the fuse*.

That was all Gus heard before he was called to his next patient, a little girl who'd lost an arm to a cluster bomblet after mistaking it for a rattle.

Later, after the brothers were gone, Gus took pencil and paper out to the yard, hoping to copy down what Adnan had drawn, but the dirt had been carefully smoothed.

That night, he sat on the edge of his bed with the radio, considering whether there was really anything to report. He'd overheard a few cryptic phrases, observed some scratching in the dirt. It might be something; then again, it might not.

He started to put the radio away, but the impulse to prove himself to Curtis was surprisingly strong. He extended the antenna, thumbed the "talk" button, and proceeded to describe the boys, down to the size and shape of their incisions.

•

Three days later, the Magheed finally returned to the village, rousting Gus from the clinic by pounding the door and shouting, "Time for your first paycheck!"

He looked like a different man. His cheeks were sunken and his beard unkempt. Gus suggested that they go shooting another day, but the Magheed insisted. "No," he said, "a marshman pays his debts."

His tone was unsettling. Gus wondered, as he climbed into the chief's canoe, along with Fennuk and two new bodyguards, whether someone had overheard him using the radio and betrayed him.

"Now," the Magheed said, when they were under way, "let's see what you can do with that cape gun."

Gus was pleased to discover that he wasn't such a bad shot after all, despite the Magheed's comments, which were always a variation on, *The pigs will sleep soundly tonight*.

They went through a pouch of slugs, then took a break from shooting, passing a canteen back and forth across the yokes as the paddlers dug in, carrying them farther and farther from shore.

The Magheed asked after some of Gus's patients, but his mind seemed to be elsewhere. "Tell me something—totally different. How is it for women in your country these days? I'm thinking of sending Thali away for a while."

"She'd do well there. She'd do well anywhere."

"You know, she hates being away from the marshes. She has me to blame for that."

"I'd be happy to write some letters, maybe help her land on her feet."

" 'Land on her feet,' " the Magheed said, "like a cat. I always liked that expression. Thali's mother taught it to me." He handed Gus another pouch. "Here, try the heron's nest on that old piling."

Gus loaded a slug, but hesitated before sighting the target.

"Don't worry. Once a heron abandons a nest, she doesn't come back."

It took four rounds to hit the nest, which finally exploded in a puff of white straw.

"Three warning shots?" the Magheed said. "The pigs will build you a statue! Now, onwards."

Once again, the paddlers dug in. Soon the canoe was beyond sight of shore. They'd entered the zone of near-perpetual fog in the center of the lake that was the source of a charming legend: the marshmen liked to imagine that it concealed a mystical floating island, a kind of Eden. The fog played tricks with sound, muffling the churning water, amplifying the paddlers' labored breathing.

The long silence made Gus uncomfortable, so he asked about the Magheed's trip.

"A bad business," he said. "I suppose you've heard that our weapons are being confiscated?"

"Major Curtis mentioned something to that effect."

"Ah, Curtis," the Magheed said. He spat into the water, then watched as bright fingerlings rose to his spittle. "His men are taking everything," he said, "not just the new rifles. Our boys don't even have enough powder to make fireworks."

"Fireworks?"

"A wedding tradition. They call it the *fountain of fire*. Basically a steel drum full of homemade rockets. The groom's family sets it off for good luck."

"I see," Gus said. He hoped his face didn't look as hot as it suddenly felt.

"But enough of that. Thali tells me you've been circumcising everything in sight."

"I can practically do it in my sleep," Gus said. "Look, I hate to do this, but I have some Gram stains I have to attend to. I'm sorry, but I need to get back."

"Of course," the Magheed said. "There's just one stop I want to make along the way."

All Gus could think about was getting to the radio and correcting his mistake about the boys, but instead of turning back, the paddlers maneuvered the canoe down an unfamiliar waterway. While Fennuk lectured Gus on the proper cleaning and maintenance of his cape gun, the Magheed brooded, trailing his fingers in the water while humming the same melancholy figure over and over again, like a musician rehearsing a difficult part. Normally, Gus would have asked about it, on the off chance the tune was significant, another bit of marsh lore he might absorb; but this time he let it go. He didn't want to say or do anything to delay their return.

Gus's spirits lifted when the canoe grounded on a sandbar. Everyone climbed out; the paddlers hoisted the boat and started to turn it. It seemed they were finally heading home, but the Magheed had other plans.

Flanked by the bodyguards, they hiked a series of weed-choked hills. At the top of the last rise, the grass thinned and then abruptly ended, revealing a village that had been burned out. Everything was gone. The ground had been baked into something like brick, dotted here and there with scorched postholes. The emptiness was shocking.

Gus raised his camera, but the Magheed stayed his arm and said, "Not here."

Fennuk and the others held back at the edge of the clearing, while the Magheed led Gus to the site of the guesthouse, now just a rectangular hearth open to the sky.

The Magheed knelt at the hearth and probed the ashes with the remains of a fire tool. "Our 'neighbor to the north,' as you called him, had used chemicals on us before," he said. "Defoliant. It made breast milk sour, ruined fodder. Very bad if you breathed the mist. But this was something new. The planes dropped canisters and . . ." He made a throat-cutting gesture with his thumb. "We found people curled up, their bones crushed by convulsions, all their fluids spilled out."

"Nerve gas?" Gus said.

The Magheed nodded. "This village," he said, "was like death in life. Right here, on top of the guesthouse, we found two roofers, a father and son, lying among bundles of thatching for a repair, holding hands. They must have known it was the end. We had to break the fingers to get them apart."

Then he stood and pointed in the direction of the bodyguards, who tossed away the cigarette they'd been passing and jumped to attention. "And over there, a hut with a little girl in the doorway, reaching out with a scrap of fish. Just lying there like she was asleep, her head on her arm. The family cat was there, too. You know, ready to take a bite. The jaws were torn open. The spine was like a corkscrew." He paused, then tossed away the fire tool before adding, "It was like that everywhere."

They walked to the communal oven, where Gus examined a puddle of slag that had once been a shovel or a peel, some tool for baking. The oven itself was still standing, but the bricks lining its floor had exploded from the heat.

"The fire was my doing," the Magheed said. "I was against it at first, but my men thought the corpses might be dangerous."

At the far edge of the village, a goat pen had somehow escaped the conflagration. The remains of a goat were chained to a post. Grass was starting to grow in the fertile muck around its bones. The Magheed rested his hand on the gate. "If it hadn't been for the foreign guns," he said, "all of our villages would look like this now."

4

When they finally beached the canoe in the shadow of the brick kiln, Gus was relieved to find there was no need for the radio after all. An enlisted man with greasy eyeglasses and a camouflage bandanna was waiting for him on the sand.

"Major Curtis requires your presence, posthaste," the soldier said, with one hand tucked in the small of his back, like a waiter, and the other extended in the direction of the launch.

Gus told him he'd be right back with his bag, but the soldier said he wouldn't be needing it. He declined to explain why not, but Gus supposed he knew.

The silent treatment continued all the way across the lake. It had been a long day, and Gus was tired and put out; the only consolation was the prospect of correcting his unfortunate mistake about the brothers. The drone of the engine, punctuated now and then by the sound of the metal hull pounding a rogue wave, was a perfect reflection of his mood. From time to time, his eyes fell shut. Once, he even fell asleep, only to be jarred awake by a dream in which his hands were reversed, the right somehow having been replaced with the left.

The squawk of a radio broke his reverie. They were approaching a hulking military barge whose deck was lined with smudge pots, some of which had just been lit. The flames cast an eerie orange glow on the pilothouse and gantry crane, even as they were slowly obscured by the pots' heavy smoke.

After a spotlight methodically swept the water, the launch was cleared to come alongside. Gus kept his eye on the crane, where the occasional glint of a telescopic sight betrayed the position of a sniper.

Curtis was waiting at the top of the rusted boarding ladder. "You're late," he said. "We already lost one of them."

Gus was led belowdecks to a hold crammed with crate after crate of rifles. The modern ones were neatly packed; the others were in a jumble, their barrels spiked. There were artillery pieces, mortars, even the odd ship's cannon, including one antique swivel piece that looked like it belonged in a maritime museum.

Beyond the weapons hold, in a vast compartment redolent of diesel and bilge, was a brig that had been improvised from shipping containers. At the sound of footsteps, a cry rose up from the prisoners. One of Curtis's men, a little fellow with pale eyes who was introduced to Gus as Gunny Reiff, had an answer to the prisoners' lament: blasts of water from a fire suppression hose, introduced into the containers, one by one, through the airholes.

Just past the containers was a row of cabins with armored doors.

"In here," Curtis said, working the hatch wheel of one of them. "We need you to confirm this was your guy."

Gus went in alone. The odor of urine was overpowering. There were two pieces of metal furniture bolted to the floor: a chair and a table. A bloody sheet covered the body on the table.

Gus pulled back the sheet. It was Adnan. They'd used the wire on him. That much was clear from the violence that had been done to his head. But something else had killed him. The blood vessels in his eyes were burst; his lips were blue.

Gus tried to continue his examination downward, but the sheet was stuck to his arm. In freeing it, Gus saw that the boy's hand was missing. The stump had been wrapped with a bright cloth, a handkerchief in high-visibility orange.

Curtis knocked impatiently, then spoke through the open door. "Well?" he said.

"It's him," Gus said. "Where's the brother?"

"Reiff's working on him."

"Tell him to stop," Gus said.

While Curtis walked him a few doors down, Gus explained his mistake. "It was stupid," he said. "I didn't know the phrase. Even so. The circumcisions. Fireworks. I should have known it was for a wedding."

Curtis shook his head. "No. You did the right thing."

"How is this remotely the right thing?"

"I've got three soldiers in the morgue from an attack on a collection point this morning. Twelve from an an ambush on a convoy last week. Where do you think these boys are getting their gunpowder?"

They stopped in front of another bulkhead. Curtis rapped with his knuckles, a signal that was returned a few moments later from inside. "Reiff's ready for you. Now go in there and do your job, Lieutenant. And let Reiff do his."

Kareem was hooded and strapped to the table, which was inclined slightly toward his head. The hood was soaking wet. Reiff was pressing it tightly to the boy's face while drizzling water on it from a kettle. As the seconds ticked by, Kareem's back arched and he began to fight the straps with all his strength. Gus moved protectively to his side, but there was nothing to do except wait.

Reiff's lips moved as he counted. He stared at the hood with great intensity, as if he could see through it.

When he finally lifted his hand, and Kareem's gasping and

retching confirmed that the timing had been just right, he turned to Gus and grinned. "I took it too far with the other one," he said. "It's a new method. New to me, anyway."

"There's something you need to know," Gus said. He told Reiff the same thing he'd told Curtis, but Reiff wasn't interested. "Not my department," he said.

"What do you mean, 'Not my department'?"

The hood turned slowly toward Gus's voice. Kareem called him *Doctor* and started to plead for help.

"You see?" Gus said. "He wants to talk. He's my patient. Give me a few minutes with him. He trusts me."

Reiff shook his head. "Tell him about his brother."

"Tell him *what* about his brother?"

"Just tell him."

Gus figured the boy had a right to know. As quietly and simply as possible, he explained that Adnan was dead.

Kareem went very still.

"Did you mention the hand?" Reiff said. "Tell him it'll happen to him, too, if he doesn't talk."

Gus shook his head. "I'm not going to be a part of this," he said.

"Say it," Reiff said, "or so help me, I'll shove his brother's hand right up his ass."

Kareem, Gus said, *please believe me. Adnan is dead.*

No, Kareem said. *No no no.*

I saw with my own eyes, Gus said. *They cut his hand. This man has proof.*

The boy cursed Gus, cursed all foreigners, shook his head fiercely, then, choking, fell back and started to cry.

"Good," Reiff said. "You got to him. Now tell him we're going to feed the body to the vultures—no, wait; say that we're going to hang it from the gantry. But be sure to mention the birds."

Gus shook his head.

Reiff flashed a prim smile. "No? Then I guess I'll just keep going."

Reiff had a way of using a rib spreader in the boy's mouth that required the hood to come off. There were surgical masks on hand for those brief occasions. Gus didn't want to cover his face. It felt villainous. He told Reiff there was no point, since Kareem already knew him from the clinic, but Reiff was a believer in protocol.

Breathing through clean linen, if only for a few minutes, gave a welcome reprieve from the stench, but each time Gus tied the familiar knot behind his head, he silently added a year of service in the marshes as his punishment. This was a way of wearing a surgical mask he'd never imagined.

At one point, when he was alone with Kareem for a few minutes, Gus loosened the hood and gingerly peeled it back. The boy's jaw hung crooked. The left side of the mandible was bulging where it had fractured. The bone had given way with a wet snap. There had been two sessions with the spreader since then.

Gus poured a bit of water in the open mouth, then slipped in some pills, aspirin he happened to have in his pocket. *Swallow*, he said. *For the pain.*

The boy spat out the pills along with several broken teeth. *No*, he said. *Unclean.*

Please, Gus said. Reiff's mincing footsteps echoed down the hall. *Quickly. Where did Adnan get the powder?*

Kareem licked his upper lip. His eyes fluttered shut. For the first time, Gus noticed his long, thick eyelashes. Marsh girls liked thick eyelashes. Thali had told him that once.

Gus resecured the hood and went to wash his hands. He kept his back to Reiff so he wouldn't see how they were shaking.

"Guess what?" Reiff said. "We're out of this shithole. You're wanted up on deck. Curtis is getting ready to make the announcement."

It was late afternoon. Gus had been below so long, the sunlight completely blinded him. He listened, swaying gently, with his eyes closed. Apparently, the invasion had begun during the night. It was unfortunate, but the marshmen had proven to be unworthy stewards of their own destiny. They'd begun using their barbaric tactics against the very forces that had helped with their liberation. The plan was to get in, dismantle this dangerous new insurgency, and get out.

Curtis thanked his men for all their hard work and sacrifice. He held up Reiff as an example of an enlisted man who, by virtue of his exemplary service, was soon to make the leap to the officer corps.

There was plenty of praise to go around. Gus was singled out for his humanitarian work at the clinic. He stood, Curtis said, as a reminder that even in an active theater of war, there was still a place for a soldier's highest aspirations.

Curtis had every intention of sending Gus back to the fleet, but Gus made the case that he'd be more useful in the field. Curtis was surprised, but he radioed ahead on Gus's behalf, then offered him a cigar.

Gus took it, then handed it back. "Save this for someone who needs it," he said.

"Suit yourself," Curtis said, propping his feet on a toolbox. If he noticed the edge in Gus's voice, he didn't show it. He was in an expansive mood. He cut the head with an old safety blade, then lit up. "I was wrong about you, Lieutenant," he said. "You've got some stones, after all."

"What will happen to the prisoners?"

"They'll be transferred to a base near the port city. Don't worry. Those guys are pros."

"And the Magheed?"

Curtis waved the cigar. "Relax," he said. "That's all been taken care of."

B y the time Gus made it back to the Magheed's village to collect his things, the sky was full of helicopters. It seemed that every bird in the marshes was on the wing, too, panicked by the thunderous demolition of the haze.

Gus found Hamza on the sand by the lagoon, polishing the barrels of the cape gun with a handful of grass. He was wearing the Magheed's headcloth. Gus had never seen Hamza in a head-cloth. It dwarfed him. He'd had to double the band to make it fit.

Come with me, Gus said, slinging the gun over his shoulder.

The Magheed got two of them with a pistol before they cut him, Hamza said. *I kept the hands, but they took the rest. Help me find him. We have to bury him.*

Gus wrapped an arm around him, but Hamza wouldn't budge.

Smoke billowed from the guesthouse. The roof had burned away, exposing the main ribs, which were smoldering. Apparently, they were too dense to burn.

Where's Thali?

Hamza shrugged and said, *Gone to look for you. She said you'd know what to do.*

We have to go, too, Gus said, shouting to make himself heard over the helicopters.

Hamza didn't seem to comprehend. He just stood there, looking from the lake to the sky, his eyes narrowed to slits by the smoke.

Gus took the boy's arm and started to pull him away from the beach. Hamza let himself be led for a few paces, then dropped to the sand and started to cry. *This is your fault*, he wailed. *Everything was fine before you came.*

Gus kept trying to lead him away, but the boy's hands were slippery from the grass he'd used to polish the gun. Its sap was thick and white. Gus wondered if it had healing properties. For a precious moment he was himself again, excited by medical curiosity.

Then one of the helicopters broke formation and headed straight for the lagoon. The staccato roar convulsed the waterfowl.

You'll be safe at the clinic, Gus said, scooping Hamza into his arms. *I promise.*

The boy's face was yellow with bruises. He resisted, even though his eyelids were drooping. Gus held him tight as he walked. He didn't know what else to do, so he hummed a tune, something his mother had sung to him as a child, in sickbed.

He'd sung it once for Thali at the end of one of their evenings together, when she was nodding off with a book in her father's reading chair. Just before leaving, he'd put a soft rug on her lap and brushed the hair from her sleeping eyes. There might have been consequences if someone had seen him leaning in to kiss her forehead, but he'd risked it anyway.

The song had the desired effect on the boy. After a while, he gave up struggling, rested his head on Gus's shoulder, and slept.

A NOTE ABOUT THE AUTHOR

Matthew Olshan is the author of several books for young readers, including *Finn*, *The Flown Sky*, and *The Mighty Lalouche*. He lives in Baltimore.